Virtue
A Fairy Tale

Amanda Hocking

Seven Fallen Hearts 1

This is a work of fiction. All of the characters,
organizations, and events portrayed in this novel are either
products of the author's imagination or are used
fictitiously.

www.HockingBooks.com

ＤEDICATION

The first stories I ever wrote were fanfiction of Labyrinth and the Muppets before I was in grade school.

The first book I ever published – My Blood Approves – I self-published to raise enough money to go to the Jim Henson Exhibit in Chicago.

The first version of Virtue I wrote because I wanted to write something that would utilize the Jim Henson Creature Shop if it ever became a movie.

So this book, along with all of my books, and my daily reminder to myself to be kind and have fun, are all dedicated to Jim Henson.

Other Books by Amanda Hocking

Seven Fallen Hearts
Virtue
Tristitia
A Hungry Heart
Superbia (Coming February 14, 2024)

My Blood Approves Saga
My Blood Approves
Fate
Flutter
Wisdom
Swear
Letters to Elise (Prequel Novella)
Little Tree (Short Story)
My Blood Approves: Complete Saga (eBook Bundle)

Trylle Saga
Switched
Torn
Ascend
Frostfire
Ice Kissed
Crystal Kingdom
The King's Games: A Short Story
The Lost City
The Morning Flower
The Ever After

ᴀᴜᴛʜᴏʀ's ɴᴏᴛᴇ

on *Virtue: Revised & Extended Edition*

The first version of *Virtue* was written in 2010-2011, when I was around twenty-six. My career had started exploding, and I was feeling happy but overwhelmed and confused. So I wanted to throw myself into the things that made me fall in love with writing in the first place – fairy tale romance and adventures with magical creatures.

That was what this book grew from, and even though I moved onto other projects over the years, a part of my heart has always lingered in the world of *Virtue*.

A little nugget of an idea grew in my brain, thinking on the world, and it finally coalesced into a full-fledged idea: a series of books and short stories – seven in total – that could show so much more of the vibrant, exciting world. *Virtue* would become the flagship novel in the Seven Fallen Hearts Saga.

Naturally, if I wanted to use *Virtue* to launch a whole new series, I needed to go back and reread it. I thought there might be a few copyedits and stylistic changes I would want to smooth out for a second edition, but I planned to leave the bulk of the story untouched.

That was, until I read it.

There are many, many things I love about *Virtue*, but there were serious issues with the way parts of the book were written. I have come so far in my own personal growth and being more aware of the language I use and how it can affect readers – particularly the teens and young adults reading them – but I didn't realize how many problematic attitudes I still had when I was in my twenties.

Some of the issues – like rather overt slut-shaming and body-shaming – were baked into the story and concept much more than I remembered, and I couldn't just make a few little tweaks and edits.

Virtue needed a full-on rewrite to fix some of the mistakes. There was plenty of sweet romance and dynamic fantasy that it was still worth saving, but it didn't need any of that malicious junk to bog it down.

So that's what I've done.

Fortunately, *Virtue* had never been a very popular book, and I had never even released it in paperback form, so I am hopeful that the original didn't do that much harm.

But one of the benefits of self-publishing is that I can change things. I don't have to leave harmful outdated ideas out in the world. I can correct them and make something more beautiful, and with any luck, it will find a way to resonate with readers.

This revised and extended version of *Virtue* is much better than the original work. I feel like the fantasy and sweetness are able to shine so much brighter without being clouded by a judgmental, puritanical ideology, and I am really pleased with how it turned out. It's a much kinder book.

I hope you all enjoy this new edition of *Virtue*, and I am very excited to show you the world of the Seven Fallen Hearts Saga.

As always, stay safe, be kind, and happy reading.

Amanda Hocking
December 5, 2021

CHAPTER ONE

THE PALACE NESTLED IN THE ROLLING HILLS of Insontia was hardly the fanciest place Lux had ever been, and honestly, it disappointed him. Everything tried so hard to be opulent and lavish, and even when it succeeded, the effort was all too apparent.

Lux had gotten through the gate with a stolen invitation to the party, and he'd been ushered down to the ballroom. Instead of going in, he waited just outside the gilded doors, spying on the masquerade ball with disdain.

The ballroom was filled to capacity. He hadn't expected that many people to attend a tacky affair like this, but once again, Lux had overestimated humanity. All the young women wore flowing gowns, and their faces were hidden by glittery masks. A brunette caught sight of him hiding in the doorway, and she lowered her mask to get a better look at him.

Lux wore a perfectly tailored suit with a black shirt underneath, the top left open to reveal a hint of chest. His blond hair had been pushed back so it lay straight, except for where the curls formed at the base of his neck. He had the kind of smile that, when used correctly, got him nearly anything he wanted.

There had been a time when an event such as this appealed to Lux. This anniversary party for a King and Queen he'd never met would've held some interest for him, even with its faux splendor and forced extravagance. The dance floor should have been a treat, full of attractive, vapid nobles to entertain him, but he could barely muster the effort to flirt.

He'd grown bored with it all.

If he hadn't been sent, Lux never would have come here. His instructions were to attend this ball, and everything would be explained once he arrived. After years of this, he'd gotten used to vague orders, and it suited him better when he didn't know what his Master was doing.

A servant offered him a flute of champagne, and Lux swallowed it down greedily before plotting his escape. He considered leaving the palace entirely, hopping on his black horse Velox, and racing off to meet Gula at a bar where they could eat and drink too much.

But he knew better than to disobey, so he settled for wandering away from the masquerade. He needed a moment to let the champagne hit him before he dealt with the crowd in the ballroom.

Lux went down a long hallway, following a burgundy carpet. Eventually, he found himself in a rotunda, the sounds of the party a faded din on the other side of the palace.

A massive chandelier hung from the ceiling, its crystals dangling like stalactites. The walls were papered in off-white with gold designs. The true centerpiece was the wide marble staircase curving up to the second story twenty feet above him.

Lux put his hands on his hips and sighed. The carpet underneath his shoes was discolored and balding, the wallpaper was peeling in the corners, and half of the candles in the chandelier were out.

2

None of this made any sense. What could his Master possibly want with a King and Queen and their fading glory in a forgotten place like Insontia?

"Are you lost?" A soft voice came from the top of the stairs, sending a warm shiver through him, and Lux turned to see a girl.

Her long, dark hair hung down her back, decorated simply with diamond clips, and her sparkling white dress left her shoulders bare. Then her rose red lips curved into the most delicate of smiles.

For a moment, he was struck completely still by her beauty, and he couldn't remember the last time that had happened to him.

"Are you all right?" she asked, a nervous undercurrent to her words. Her hands were on the banister, and she leaned forward to see him better.

"Yes, I'm fine." He found his voice and flashed her a charming smile, and she returned it easily as her shoulders relaxed. "I needed some air." He stepped toward the stairs, feeling oddly drawn to her, but he stopped himself before going farther. "What about you? Are you lost?"

"No." She gave a small laugh and lowered her eyes, her hands twisting absently on the railing. "I know my way around here quite well."

"You're not enjoying the party either?" Lux asked.

"The party is lovely, but I am an awkward guest." She gave him a sheepish smile. "I feel silly shouting down to you. Shall I come down to meet you?"

"Yes," Lux replied before she'd even finished the question.

She descended the stairs with a quick elegance, nearly gliding down them. Her fingers trailed along the banister, and her gown flowed out behind her.

3

Something about her was unnervingly captivating. He didn't trust himself to even look at her, so he ran a hand through his hair and pretended to admire the chandelier.

"Do you like it?" she asked when she reached him.

"What?" Lux allowed himself to glance over at her. Up close, she was even lovelier, and he had to remind himself to breathe.

"The chandelier." She gestured to it.

"It's … nice," Lux said noncommittally, afraid of offending her.

"Queen Scelestus commissioned it when she married the King," she said, and Lux noticed a sadness in her tone. "She wanted to leave her imprint on the palace."

"Well, she certainly has," Lux muttered, letting his derision seep into his words. She laughed, a light sound that rippled through him. "Sorry. I don't even know your name."

"Lily."

"I'm Lux."

Then she held her hand out to him, and he bent down and kissed the back of it. Her skin was cool on his lips, and her cheeks flushed ever so slightly.

"The ball doesn't suit you either?" she asked when he reluctantly released her hand. She took a step away, and he followed after her.

"No. I'm not much into parties," Lux lied. He'd spent the majority of his existence partying, but he wanted to find common ground with her, desperate to find any reason at all to extend the conversation.

"There are too many people." Lily linked her hands together in front of her, resting them on the embroidered bodice of her dress. "And they all stare at me."

"I don't blame them." He took another step closer to her, so close that he imagined he could smell the sweet fragrance of her skin. "If I may be so bold, you look radiant in that dress. In fact, I would say that no one has ever appeared more luminescent than you do right now."

"That's not true at all." She shook her head, making her dark waves sway around her. The rose on her cheeks deepened, and her smile turned shy.

She lifted her head to look at him, maybe to protest further, but as soon as her eyes met his, all her words died on her lips. His heart pounded in his chest.

And then she closed the distance between them, and all at once, her mouth was crashing against his.

He kissed her back, without hesitation. Even though he was caught off guard, he lost himself in her immediately, and he pulled her to him. She threw her arms around his neck, and as she kissed him, she wrapped the curls of his hair around her finger.

That simple gesture did something to him he couldn't explain, and he froze. His heart even ceased to beat.

Lily had noticed his abrupt change and stopped kissing him. Her dark eyes searched his. She moved back from him, and even though he wanted to hold her still, he couldn't seem to make his arms work as she shamefully whispered, "That was very wrong of me."

Lux shook his head, but his words came out feeble. "No."

"I'm such a fool." She put her hand to her forehead, as if in pain, and her cheeks blanched. "I hope you'll accept my humblest apologies. I have no idea what I was …" She trailed off, stepping away from him as she spoke.

"No, you've done nothing wrong." He held his hand out to her in an empty gesture.

"I should get back to the ball." Her words came out in a hurried jumble, doing a poor job of masking her quiver. "I do hope that you'll forgive my parents for raising such an obscene child."

"You're not —" He didn't have a chance to stop her before she lifted her skirts and dashed away, running down the hall toward the ballroom.

Lux wanted to chase after her, but his head was swimming. Everything felt so off-kilter. His hand went to the back of his neck, gingerly touching where she had twirled her fingers.

When his hair got a bit long, it tended to curl where it touched the top of his spine. He'd been with so many people, and one of them had to have played with his hair. It *had* to have happened, at least once.

But nothing had ever struck him as forcefully as when Lily had done that.

Before he could ponder things further, a small man interrupted. He came out of a doorway hidden in the wall, pushing it open so soundlessly that if Lux hadn't been looking, he wouldn't have noticed him at all.

The man was very tiny, almost impish, with slender arms and high cheekbones. His gray eyes appeared too large for his dirt-smudged face, and scraggly hair fell across his forehead.

He limped toward Lux, favoring his right leg.

"You are the one they call Lux?" The man bent low, looking up to inspect Lux.

"I am." Lux raised an eyebrow. "I'm to have business with you?"

"Not with me. With my Mistress," he clarified. "I'm merely her servant, Jinn."

"I see," Lux said, but he still wasn't convinced that his Master would want anything from people like these. Admittedly, Lux had done business with far worse people in far worse places, but it was always for a very good reason. Here, he couldn't see what any of them had to offer.

Well, that wasn't completely true. He glanced back down the hall, after Lily, and for her sake, he hoped he wouldn't see her again.

"Come along, then," Jinn waved Lux on, hobbling toward the grand staircase. "She's expecting us, and she doesn't like to be kept waiting."

CHAPTER TWO

LUX GAVE JINN A WIDE BERTH before following him up
the stairs. The small servant smelled of frogs and
toadstools, a common side effect of having a
sorceress for a Mistress. That made a bit more sense.
Sorcery was something Lux's Master had a hand in.

At the top of the stairs, Jinn took a left down
another long hallway. They went past several closed
doors before Jinn pushed open a secret door hidden
behind a painting of a dark horse.

Jinn held the door open, offering a grin that
revealed a missing tooth, and Lux slid past him into a
secret chamber. Black silk draped the walls, adding a
macabre elegance to the dark room. Iron sconces were
dotted among the drapes, bathing the room with dim
yellow light, and two red velvet couches with gold
claw feet rested against the walls.

It was the massive mirror on the far wall that
caught Lux's attention. That, and the table below,
lined with vials, pouches, and alchemy jars. Directly
beside it sat a large black cauldron. and the air reeked
of toadstool and potions.

This must be where the magic happens, Lux
thought.

He was about to ask Jinn where his Mistress was
when he saw a shimmer in the black silk on the walls
and realized that it wasn't the drapery. Her gown
blended in seamlessly, and he had a feeling that it had

9

more to do with a cloaking spell than it did with her designer.

She turned to face him, the dark folds of her dress cascading around her. The bodice clung tightly to her body, pushing up her low-cut assets. Her black hair had been pulled back severely, and despite her best efforts of makeup and magic, time had obviously begun catching up with her. Not that she wasn't strikingly beautiful. If Lux hadn't been so flustered by the kiss stolen moments ago, he'd most certainly have attempted to seduce the sorceress.

"Lux, I presume." She smiled at him with her lips blood red. The wicked decadence of it ignited something inside him. Or it would have, if he could shake the taste of Lily from his lips.

"At your service." Lux flashed her a dazzling smile, and he was pleased to see it had some effect on her. Her cheeks flushed slightly, and her long eyelashes fluttered.

"I am Queen Scelestus, and this is my home." She gestured expansively to the area around her, but she did it with a sneer. "I trust you found the ball satisfactory."

"Satisfactory is one way to describe it," Lux replied dryly.

Scelestus threw back her head and laughed. It was a truly dark cackle, the kind he'd always been partial to. His interest in her piqued, but the usual hunger inside him remained strangely dormant.

"It was my husband's idea," she said wearily and sat back on one of the sofas, spreading her gown out around her. "He is such a bore. As if fifteen long years in this palace is anything to celebrate."

Jinn hobbled across the room to where a cantor and several glasses sat on a small table. He poured a dark shimmering liquid into stout snifters and brought one over to the Queen first, then Lux.

He took the glass willingly, but before drinking, he sniffed it. The liquid smelled of brandy and fire, but that only meant that he couldn't smell the poison, not that there wasn't any.

"You don't trust me." A corner of her mouth curved up as she watched him inspecting his glass. In response, he threw back the drink in one gulp, and she laughed loudly.

"Thank you." He handed his empty snifter back to Jinn, then sat down on the sofa across from Scelestus. "Shall we get down to business?"

"Yes, I suppose we'd better," Scelestus said with a scowl. "I have to get back to that dreadful party before they notice I'm missing. Did your Master explain what you're to do?"

"No. He's left you to fill me in." Lux crossed his leg over his knee and settled more into the couch.

"Good." She twirled her snifter absently in her hand, watching as the light refracted through the glass and remaining liquid. "It's very important that we keep this all quiet, at least until everything is finished. My husband must never find out. I told Valefor to send the one he trusted the most, and he sent me you."

"For good reason." Lux let his pride sharpen his smile. "I keep my secrets."

"Excellent." Scelestus looked at him directly. "You are to take a girl to Valefor."

"That's all?" Lux raised an eyebrow. He'd been expecting a task far more difficult or scandalous. If there was one thing he excelled at, it was getting someone to leave a party with him. "I don't need to deliver a payment to you?"

"No, Valefor will take care of that part himself." She smoothed out the silk of her dress and sat up straighter. "It's absolutely imperative that he receive her as soon as possible, and he wants her in mint condition."

She stressed the "mint" part, and while that might be a bit of an inconvenience for him, he could manage. He didn't have to romance every young woman he charmed to leave with him, although it certainly made things more fun when he did.

"Done," Lux said. "Now who is this lucky young lady?"

"My stepdaughter, Lily."

His breath caught in his throat, but he managed to keep his smile in place. His hand twitched, wanting to go to the nape of his neck, to touch the hair Lily had twirled around her fingers, but he balled it into a fist at his side.

"Is that a problem?" Scelestus eyed him suspiciously.

"No, of course not." He shook his head and swallowed down the sick feeling growing inside him.

"She's down in the ballroom somewhere, probably hiding in a corner. She keeps to herself." Scelestus didn't try to mask the disgust in her voice. "She has on a white gown, long dark hair. She's quite pretty, I've been told, not that she ever has any suitors." The Queen snorted at that. "She's as timid and dull as a field mouse. Just like her father."

"It shouldn't be too hard to get her away then," Lux heard himself saying, and he was grateful that his words sounded normal and didn't belie the panic he felt.

"I wouldn't think so. She's a half-wit, at best." The Queen shrugged. "Be sure you don't make a scene. I thought a party would be the best way for her to slip out unnoticed. By the time her father realizes what's happening, it will be too late." She smiled again, the wicked one he suddenly found revolting.

"What does Valefor want with her?" Lux asked.

He shouldn't even be asking. As often as he could, he avoided knowing what his Master did. It made his work so much easier that way.

"Whatever it is he wants with any stupid girl, I suppose." Scelestus shook her head, as if it hadn't even occurred to her what someone like Valefor would do with her timid stepdaughter. "You know better than I the things that your Master desires."

"That I do." Lux breathed deeply and tried to remind himself that this didn't matter. That *she* didn't matter. His purpose in life had nothing to do with Lily or her well-being.

"I should return to the ball." Scelestus sighed and got to her feet. "And you should find Lily before the attendance starts to dwindle."

Lux stood up. "Yes, of course."

"Do you know how to get back to the ballroom? It's best if we don't return together."

"Yes, I do," he lied.

He didn't feel certain of anything. In the course of half an hour, everything had turned upside down, and he needed a moment to collect his thoughts. But Scelestus expected him to do his job, and more importantly, so did Valefor.

His Master Valefor was the last one in all of Cormundie he wanted to upset. That meant Lux must do what he was told, the same as he always had.

Since deciding to serve him, Lux tried not to second-guess anything his Master asked of him. Some of the things he did weren't pleasant, but that was the price he paid. The price he had *chosen* to pay.

As he walked out of Queen Scelestus's secret chambers, Lux found himself fearing that, for the first time, he might not be able to follow through with his orders. All because a beautiful princess had stolen a kiss and wrapped his hair around her finger.

CHAPTER THREE

IN THE BALLROOM, everyone danced in time with the music. The gowns twirled around the women, shimmering and swaying in the light. They linked arms with their partners, using their free hands to hold the masks in front of their faces, while the spectators on the fringe watched with fascination. It all seemed a little too entrancing, and Lux wondered whether a spell from Scelestus had anything to do with their fervent interest.

He waited at the edge of the dancefloor, and his gaze immediately went to Lily, hiding on the far side of the room. No one else seemed to notice her, even though he found her to be the loveliest one there. Her eyes were on the floor, but she softly swayed to the music.

From the corner of his eye, he could see Queen Scelestus seated beside her husband, King Adriel. Lux had held some hope that Lily's father would notice something amiss, but he wore the same goofy, mesmerized grin as everyone else.

It was only Lux that stood in the way of whatever his Master had planned for Lily. All he had to do to protect her was to stay away from her… and then she looked up, her dark eyes catching his from across the ballroom.

She smiled at him. A quick glimpse of one, before an embarrassed shade of crimson highlighted her cheeks, and she looked away.

15

He plummeted into the packed ballroom floor, clumsily pushing the dancers aside. Going around the edge of the room would've been less obtrusive, but it wouldn't be as fast, and he didn't want to waste a moment away from her.

Finally, he reached her, in the quiet corner. Behind him, the revelers had returned to their dancing, as if they'd never even noticed the small scene he'd created. Somehow in the bustling party, it felt like it was only him and Lily.

"You're not dancing," Lux said as he stood before her, and she stared up at him with her wide eyes.

"Neither are you." Her voice was even, but the heavy rise and fall of her chest gave away her heightened emotions.

"I didn't have a suitable partner." He smiled at her, and she lowered her gaze again.

"I am certain that someone such as you could find one."

"I believe I have." He held out his hand to her, knowing he'd feel better if he had her hand in his.

She shook her head demurely and didn't take his offering. "I don't know how to dance."

"You don't dance, you don't enjoy parties. What do you like, Lily?" he asked. He'd meant to sound playful, to put her at ease, but he landed more on solemn curiosity, because he did want to know how he could make her happy.

"No, it's not that I don't like dancing or parties," she corrected him, and she lifted her eyes to hold his, raising her chin with a hint of defiance. "It's that I don't know how to dance, and I don't have any friends at this party. I'd rather not make a fool of myself and embarrass my family any further, so I prefer to keep to the shadows."

He arched his eyebrow in genuine surprise. "You don't know how to dance? Aren't all princesses educated on the fine arts of ballroom etiquette?"

"I don't know about other princesses –" she said, then under her breath, "– I don't know any other princesses." Her eyes flashed over to where the King and Queen sat, entranced by the ball. "My father only wants to keep me safe, and Queen Scelestus is too busy for my education. Most of my time is spent alone, with books, and I've read about many an exquisite dance, but they are never instructional."

"What if... what if I showed you the steps?" he asked. "Away from all the prying eyes. Outside, the moon is bright and the air is clear. I could give you a private lesson."

He gave her his most alluring smile, and she hesitated. She chewed her bottom lip, and he suddenly felt nervous that she might say no. When was the last time he'd been rejected from someone he attempted to charm?

"Please, Lily." He held his hand out to her again. "Dance with me."

This time, she took it. Her eyes were unabashedly hopeful, and it pulled at something inside him. Her hand felt small and cool in his, her skin softer than satin. He wanted to take her into his arms and return her stolen kiss from earlier in the night, but that was not what his Master wanted.

She followed him without question, and her naivety upset him. Normally he liked anything that made his job easier, but someone this innocent wouldn't last long with Valefor. Lux pushed the thought from his mind and quickened his pace. She

hurried along behind him, lifting the length of her
dress to keep from tripping.

Outside, the air felt chillier than he expected, and
when he looked at Lily, her bare shoulders were
dimpled from the cold.

"Maybe this was a bad idea. The night is rather
frosty," he said, denying his strongest urges.

In the moonlight, Lily was so beautiful and
sanguine. Her eyes were wide and glistening, and her
soft lips were pulled into a smile.

"If we dance, won't it warm me?" she asked.

He smiled then, unable to help himself. "Yes.
How silly of me."

Her hand was still in his, and when he moved
close to her, she held his gaze. He slipped his free
hand onto her waist, and she pressed herself against
him as he moved it to the small of her back.

"Put your hand on my shoulder," he told her, and
he didn't even know why he was doing it. He didn't
need to dance with her. He should be trying to leave.
But then her hand rested warmly on his shoulder, and
he was smitten.

"Good," he said, and he instructed her on a few
basic moves – a side-to-side step with a turn or two to
pull her closer to him.

"How am I doing?" she asked.

"You're perfect," he said.

At that, Lily beamed. The smallest compliment
from him, and her entire face lit up.

He licked his lips and asked her, "Why did you
kiss me?"

She blushed and immediately looked away, but
she stayed in his arms. "You have my deepest
apologies for my earlier behavior. That is very unlike
me. I … I lost myself for a moment."

"I don't want an apology," he reassured her, and he caressed the back of her hand with his thumb. "But I am curious."

"I've never had a kiss before," she admitted quietly. "And you looked... like you'd be nice to kiss. And I worried that I would never have a chance to kiss anyone."

"Why would you ever worry that?" he asked, genuinely perplexed.

"I turned eighteen last week, and I have never had any suitors or even a friend outside of my handmaids." She frowned. "I must sound so pathetic, but it's not that I never wanted more. My father keeps me safe, locked away from everything."

Pathetic wasn't the word he thought of, but her life sounded lonely. That Lux understood all too well, since he had hardly a friend himself. At least he had far more freedom than Lily seemed to have, hidden away in her ivory tower.

"You're not locked up right now," Lux pointed out, and she smiled up at him again, her face alight.

"No, I am not."

They weren't even dancing any longer. He was just holding her in his arms, alone in the courtyard under the bright moonlight.

"You're not happy here. Why don't we go somewhere you can be happy?" he asked, and his heart hammered in his chest. He was terrified she would say no, and horrified at the thought that she may say yes.

He wanted nothing more than to take her away from all this, but so he could take her back to his bed, not offer her up to his Master.

"Where will we go?" Lily asked.

"We'll decide on the way."

She was still smiling when she nodded. "Okay. Take me away from here."

CHAPTER FOUR

AS THEY RACED DOWN THE ROAD on the back of Lux's
horse Velox, with Lily's arms tight around his waist
and her head resting on his back, it occurred to him
that she may have put a spell on him.

They had been riding for some time, no
destination in mind besides away from the palace of
Insontia. The whole journey, he had been relishing the
way her arms felt around him and trying to figure out
how to keep Lily away from his Master without either
of them incurring his wrath.

But then Lux thought about how strange this all
was. He did not lose himself over a kiss from any man
or woman, no matter how attractive or charming they
might be. So what was happening to him now?

When she kissed him, perhaps she'd used some
kind of protection spell. If she had gotten word that
her stepmother was up to something devious, she
could have thought to enchant the man sent to harm
her.

That would be rather clever, and it would explain
why she'd left with him so easily.

The longer they rode, the more certain of it he
became, but he didn't know if it mattered. He still
wanted to hold Lily and kiss her and protect her.

"Where are we going?" Lily asked, her soft
words in his ear.

"You can drop the act," Lux blurted out, hoping
to startle her into admitting she cast a hex on him.

21

"What?"

"I know you put a spell on me."

"I-I don't know what you're talking about," Lily stammered and her arms loosened around him. "I'm not sure what's happened to you, but I've had nothing to do with it."

Lux slowed his horse to a stop, and he felt a pang at upsetting her. He looked back over his shoulder at her. "You truly did not enchant me with a kiss?"

"No! I have no idea what you're talking about," she insisted. "I kissed you because I wanted to, even though I know I was a silly fool and a stupid girl, just as Queen Scelestus always said."

He winced. "No, Lily. You're not a fool or stupid. You shouldn't talk about yourself like that."

"Please, just take me home," Lily said, and her voice sounded thick with tears. "I want to go home and forget this whole night."

He looked up at the night sky, so cold and far away, and he took a fortifying breath. "No. I can't do that."

"Then I will take myself." She let go of him, and he felt her moving around behind him.

"Lily," he said, but it was too late. She dismounted ungracefully, falling from the horse onto the road. "Lily!"

He leapt down, landing beside her, and he took her hand to help her to her feet. "Are you all right?"

"I am, but you don't need to worry about me. I can find my way home."

"You can't go home," he told her emphatically.

"Why not?" she asked.

"Queen Scelestus hired me to kill you," he confessed, which was close enough to the truth. Lily's eyes widened but she didn't take her hand from his.

"I can't do it. I won't hurt you," he promised her.

"Then where are you taking me?"

He shook his head. "I can't take you *anywhere*."

His Master would be able to find them. Valefor had plenty of minions and servants who were great at tracking down what he wanted. If Lily stayed with Lux, his Master would find them and torture them both.

"So you're going to leave me in the Necrosilvam?" she asked.

"Is that where we are?" He'd been so focused on Lily, he hadn't been paying attention to the scenery. He glanced around at the dark trees surrounding the road. All the branches were leafless and bare, the way they always were in the Necrosilvam. "This is the cursed forest."

The wood behind them echoed and groaned, as if waiting to swallow them up.

His Master was very good at tracking things he wanted, but other magic clouded his. The dark magic of the cursed Necrosilvam would be enough to block Valefor's usual methods, but he was still adept at finding his servants.

If Lux stayed with Lily, he would put a larger target on the Princess's back. To be safe, she should go without him.

He looked down at her and held both her hands in his. "Do you trust me?"

"I... I don't know," she said.

"Do you believe me when I say Queen Scelestus hired me to kill you?"

"Yes."

"Do you believe that I don't want to hurt you?"

She hesitated, but she finally said, "Yes."

"I can't protect you, but I think the forest can."

"The Necrosilvam?" She was aghast. "I'll be
eaten alive."

"No, you won't. You'll be cloaked, too." He took
off his jacket and wrapped it around her shoulders.
"Whatever is in that forest is far better than what
awaits if I take you with me. Keep watch at night, and
sleep during the day. Stay to the ground in the dark
and go to the trees during the light. You only need to
stay away for a few days."

That should be enough time for him to find a
replacement. There had to be another sheltered
Princess that could meet his Master's needs.

"And then go where?" Lily asked.

"You said your father wanted to keep you safe?"
he asked. "Would he protect you against the Queen of
the palace?"

She considered it and nodded. "I think so."

"Then in three days' time, go to him and tell him
she hired me to kill you," Lux said. "Tell him I
kidnapped you. Tell him anything you need to so you
can stay alive."

"Will I ever see you again?" she asked.

He swallowed down his regret. "If all goes well,
no. You won't."

He wanted to kiss her, but he knew if he did, he
would never leave her. He got on his horse without
saying a word, and he glanced back at her only once.
She stood on the side of the road in her white ball
gown with his jacket wrapped tightly around her, and
then she turned and disappeared into the forest.

Lily stood a much better chance against some
cursed trees than she did against Valefor. Lux raced
off into the night, with an ache in his chest that only
grew larger the farther he got from Lily.

CHAPTER FIVE

LILY SLID HER ARMS THROUGH THE SLEEVES of Lux's jacket, the cuffs hanging over her hands. The dead trees around her seemed to breathe and reach their branches for her. She crouched low to the ground, out of their grasp, and she convinced herself that it was all in her imagination. Trees didn't assault and kidnap girls, no matter what superstitions might claim.

Her mother always told her not to be afraid, because Lily had a powerful heart. But she'd never felt powerful, especially not since her mother died. Every day since then, she had only felt smaller and weaker.

Most of Lily's life had been spent in her bedroom, with only her handmaids and nursemaid Nancilla as company. Well, them, and Polly and Poppy. They were a pair of field mice she'd found as babies in a nest under her mattress, and she'd hand raised them.

Who would care for them now? Nancilla most likely would, if Queen Scelestus didn't kill them.

"Oh, you foolish, stupid girl," she cursed herself. "You didn't think of Polly and Poppy when you ran off with a stranger because he'd been handsome."

Only she knew that wasn't entirely the truth. Yes, Lux was very handsome, but she didn't run up kissing any good-looking man that crossed her path. There had been something about him, something almost familiar...

When she looked into his eyes, she felt a flicker of recognition, and she'd been drawn to him. She had wanted to kiss him, but it also felt like something more than that. Like she was *meant* to kiss him.

Lily put her hand to her lips, as if she'd still feel him there.

"He should've given me a kiss goodbye," she whispered to herself.

But Lux was gone, never to be seen again, and she was alone in the dark cursed wood. Her stepmother wanted her dead – which was sadly not even surprising – and if Lily survived the Necrosilvam, she'd still have to face Queen Scelestus.

One of the branches tangled in her long hair, and when she tried to pull her locks free, they only caught more. Above her, she could see the branch in the moonlight, making a fist to grab her more tightly. All the trees around her were leaning in, moving closer to her, their wood creaking and groaning as they reached for her.

She managed to escape the branch's grasp, but only by painfully leaving a lock of her hair behind. Running ahead did no good, since trees were all around her. The wind whipped through them, sounding all too much like laughter.

With branches and trees blocking her path, Lily fell to her knees. The mud and moss dampened her gown. She pulled Lux's jacket up over her head – the only protection she had – and she curled up in a ball as the branches scraped down her back.

Then abruptly, everything stopped.

The trees rasped as they straightened back into place. Lily peered out from under the jacket, uncertainly scanning the woods. She waited, fearing some kind of trap, but when there was none, she slowly got to her feet.

The forest had fallen silent around her. Nothing moaned or breathed. Even the wind was still, and the movement in her peripheral vision had stopped.

Moonlight illuminated everything around her, and while it still didn't feel "safe" in the Necrosilvam, everything had shifted. The trees seemed to be ignoring her.

Pulling Lux's jacket more tightly around her, Lily walked on. Whether things wanted to kill her or not, it wouldn't do her any good to wait around. She had no intention of living in this cursed place forever, and she had to get somewhere safer to rest.

When she had been running from the trees, her shoes had slipped off. She considered going back to look for them, but all the trees looked the same. She couldn't tell where she'd lost them, or where the road was, or even if she'd been here before. Her only plan was to keep moving until she couldn't move anymore.

The ground squished underneath her bare feet, and sometimes, she swore she felt it move. A shiver ran down her spine, and she walked faster.

The temperature continued to drop, her feet were covered in muck, and she just wanted to go home. She let her mind wander back to the brief but intense kiss she'd shared with Lux, since it seemed to be the only thing that warmed her, and she wasn't paying enough attention to the ground in front of her. Her feet slipped in something wet, and Lily stumbled forward.

She put her hands out in front of her to break the fall, and her palm caught on a gnarled root that stuck out of the ground, slicing open her hand. She winced, holding it up in the moonlight to see a thin line of blood running down her arm.

Almost instantly, Lily heard the flurry of things moving about. Once again, she had the sense of things that she couldn't quite see. She pressed the jacket against her cut to stop the bleeding and tried to keep her eyes on the shadows that moved around her.

At least the trees weren't reaching out for her again. They remained stoic, watching her spin around.

"I know you're out there!" Lily shouted as if it were some kind of threat.

The sound of wings flapping echoed off the forest around her. She looked back to see a dark creature descending toward her. At first glance, it appeared to be a simple crow, but the closer it got to her, the more she saw how little it resembled any bird she'd seen before.

It had a long, bony beak filled with tiny, jagged teeth. At the bend in its wings were leathery hands with long, sharp claws. A wriggling, serpentine tail whipped the air, and dark, mangy fur covered its body in place of feathers.

Lily ran as the horrible beast flew at her, its voice sounding like a cross between a caw and a growl. It got close enough to beat its horrible leather wings at her, so she covered her head with her arms. Its claws scraped at the back of her jacket, and then suddenly, it fell back.

But unlike the trees, it didn't completely give up its pursuit. It merely faltered for a moment.

She tripped again, and Lily couldn't help but believe the trees had done it on purpose this time, raising their roots so she would fall. The bird creature landed on the ground behind her, giving its wings one final flap for good measure, and she turned to face her attacker.

It crouched on the ground, looking as if it meant to pounce on her. A long, narrow tongue flicked out of its mouth, meaning to taste her, but she scrambled out of the way just in time.

"I'm not afraid of you!" Lily lied, as her fingers raked the forest floor in search of a defense. Finally, she found a heavy stick on the ground, and she wrapped her hand securely around it.

The bird creature stepped toward her, its talons moving lightly on the mud. Before it could get any closer, she swung the stick out. It collided hard with the creature's head, but it lay on its back for a moment, dazed by her attack, and Lily hurried to stand. It shook its head, then hopped back up on its feet.

"I don't want to hurt you," she said, holding the stick out in front of her. "So please, go away. Don't make me hit you again."

The bird creature eyed her up, staying out of the range of her stick, and then it lowered its head and let out a horrible squawk. Then she heard the flurry of wings.

The bird creature had called all of its friends. About a dozen of them had circled around her, sitting in the trees, their beady eyes glowing red in the moonlight. Some of them hissed at her, flicking their slithering tongues. Worse still, the creature on the ground seemed to be the smallest of them, and it was at least three times the size of a housecat.

"I don't want to hurt any of you! But I will! So I suggest you all fly away!" Lily yelled. Her voice quavered a little, but she hoped they didn't notice.

The creature on the ground leapt at her. She swung the stick at it, hitting it in the head again, and the others swarmed at her. She waved the stick erratically over her head, defending herself as she stepped backward. Claws and beaks stung at her arms and neck.

"Be gone with you!" A voice echoed through the trees behind Lily, followed by a crackling sound. Blue sparks flashed around her, and for a brief moment, the hair stood up on her arms.

The creatures scattered. They all squawked and hissed their disapproval, but they didn't seem willing to fight. A few of them lingered, hoping they stood a chance at getting a piece of Lily, and blue sparks snapped out again.

Finally, they all flew away, their tails flapping angrily behind them, and Lily turned around to see her protector.

She could only see the dark brown cloak and the slender arm holding a twisted rod. Lily had seen only one like it before — when she had been snooping in her stepmother Scelestus's things — but she recognized it as a magic wand.

"Thank you." Lily smiled and breathed a sigh of relief. "I don't know what I would have done if you hadn't come along."

"You shouldn't be in the woods," the woman said, the cloak still hiding her face. "You should get home."

"But I can't go home."

"I suppose right now, you are not safe travelling alone in the Necrosilvam," the woman said, sounding weary. "Follow me." Without waiting for a response, she turned her back to Lily and walked in the opposite direction.

With little other option, Lily followed her.

CHAPTER SIX

NEITHER SAID ANYTHING as they made their way through the brambles. They pushed through a prickly patch of elderberry bushes, and then Lily could see the soft glow of firelight through windows. A small cottage sat in the middle of a clearing. Smoke plumed out from the stone chimney that protruded from the thatch roof, and a twisted apple tree grew in front, the only thing in the whole forest with leaves.

"You live *here*?" Lily gasped. "In the Necrosilvam?"

"It's quiet," the woman said, as if that answer made sense, and went into the house.

Lily entered through the small wooden door and found the one-room cottage surprisingly cozy. A fire burned brightly in the hearth, and a small black cauldron rested over it. A wooden table with two chairs sat by the front door, along with a row of cupboards and a wash basin that served as the kitchen. A bed was in the corner, much smaller than the one the Princess slept on at home. Vials, jars, pouches littered every shelf that lined the walls and every spare inch of the counter. The whole place smelled of her stepmother's servant Jinn, but Lily didn't know exactly what it was.

"Thank you so much for rescuing me," Lily said, shutting the door behind her.

31

"What were you doing out there?" The woman slipped off her cloak, tossing it on her faded bedspread.

She went over to stir the cauldron, keeping her back to Lily. Her long cinnamon hair had been pulled back in a braid, but most of it had come loose, falling in a frayed mess about her head. Her dress was dirty and baggy, but the stitching and style showed that it had once been quite lovely.

"I'm not sure exactly." Lily looked down at her hands, touching at the scratch on her palm.

"You're not sure?" the woman asked dubiously and finally turned to look at her.

Lily was surprised to realize that this hermit woman was fairly young, not even as old as her stepmother, and underneath the dirt smudges and tangles of hair, she had an elegance about her. Her features were delicate but striking, almost pixie-like.

The woman sighed. "You're hurt." She scooped water from the cauldron into a small bowl and grabbed a cloth, then came over to Lily. "Take off your jacket and sit down, so I can tend to your wounds."

"Thank you," Lily said again and slipped off Lux's jacket. She meant to set it down somewhere, but the woman's nose wrinkled in disgust.

"This reeks of brimstone!" the woman snapped and snatched the jacket from Lily. She sniffed it more deeply. "Where did you get this?"

"I-I didn't smell anything," Lily stammered, unwilling to tell her about Lux after a reaction like that.

"Of course not. You're not attuned to that sort of thing." She shoved the jacket back at Lily, who took it uncertainly.

Lily held it close to her and sniffed it, but she didn't smell any brimstone, not that she really knew what that smelled like. The only scent it had was *Lux*: soft and sweet like sandalwood, but smoky and crisp, like an autumnal bonfire. She breathed it again, and warmth flooded over her as she thought of kissing him.

"Don't smile like that," the woman said, not unkindly. Lily had unwittingly started grinning at the memory of Lux, and she hurried to erase it. "Whoever gave you that jacket doesn't deserve your smiles."

"Sorry," Lily mumbled. The woman gestured for her to sit down, and she took the seat across from her.

"The brimstone does explain why you hadn't already been eaten alive by the charuns." She took Lily's hand, cleaning her wound of dirt. Lily cringed, expecting it to sting, but the hot water from the cauldron only soothed her pain. "The jacket deterred them until the scent of your blood overrode everything else."

"*Charuns?*"

"The bird-goblin creatures that attacked you in the forest."

"What does brimstone do to them?" Lily asked.

"Nothing. They just know better than to bother with anyone who stinks of it." Once she had finished cleaning the cut on Lily's hand, she turned her attention to the claw marks on her neck. She tilted Lily's head, wiping the cloth along her skin, and then studied Lily's face for a moment. "You live at the palace, don't you?"

"Yes." Lily tried to look at her, but the woman held her face at an angle. "I mean, I did."

"You're running away?"

"No." Lily sighed, unsure of how to explain what happened. She didn't want to talk about Lux, not after how the woman had reacted to his jacket. "I mean, yes. Kind of. I never fit in there. So I decided to run away."

"You ventured through the Necrosilvam because you didn't fit in?" She stopped cleaning Lily's neck and eyed her suspiciously.

"Yes," the Princess insisted weakly.

"You're Cass's daughter, aren't you?"

Lily's eyes shot up, and she gaped at the woman. "You knew my mother?"

"We were friends for a time." The woman shifted in her seat and wouldn't meet Lily's gaze.

"What's your name? Maybe I've heard of you," Lily said.

"I doubt that. You were so young when she died," she said, then sighed. "My name is Wick."

"Wick?" Lily furrowed her brow, thinking. Her mother had been dead for over fifteen years, and it'd been so long since anybody even talked about her. "I'm sorry. I don't remember."

Wick gave her a wry smile. "I think she kept me secret."

"Because you're a witch?" Lily asked.

"That is one of the reasons, yes."

"How did you know my mother?" Lily pressed.

"Oh, it was so long ago." The witch shook her head dismissively. "I don't think I even remember anymore."

"Oh, please!" Lily begged. "No one ever tells me about her. My stepmother has all but banished her name!"

Wick scowled at that and leaned back in her chair. "Cass was very kind and an eternal optimist."

She stared at the bowl of water, absently running her finger along the brim. "Far too trusting, though. That was her downfall."

"I suspect that will be mine as well." Lily looked down at the jacket in her lap, the one she found herself clinging to regardless of all logic.

"Not if you learn from your mistakes," Wick said, and with that she stood, effectively ending the conversation. "But it's getting late. That's enough talk for tonight. You have your journey home in the morning."

"But I can't go home," Lily insisted. "Not yet."

Lux had told her to wait three days to be safe, but she didn't know how to explain that to Wick. Thankfully, the witch didn't ask her anymore about it. All she said was a gruff, "We'll talk about it in the morning."

Wick threw the cloth in with a pile of rags and dumped the bowl back into the cauldron. She told Lily to take the bed, and though Lily tried to decline, the witch insisted. Lily slipped off her dress and stripped down to her slip. The bed felt lumpy and rough, but she didn't complain. She slid underneath the tattered quilt, feeling only relief at having a warm, safe place to lie.

Though her eyelids were already getting heavy, Lily watched as Wick lowered the fire and locked up the cottage. There was no other bed, and Lily didn't know where she planned on sleeping, but she found herself asking about something else entirely.

"How did you know I was my mother's daughter?" Lily asked, suppressing a yawn.

"You look just like her." Wick glanced over at her. "Now get some rest."

Lily pulled the covers more securely around her and drifted off to sleep.

CHAPTER SEVEN

THE KING OF INSONTIA DIDN'T NOTICE his daughter was missing until morning, and that was longer than Scelestus had hoped for. Her spell on the ballroom last night had kept everyone from noticing Lux abscond with the Princess, but it had worked too well. The ball ran later than any other before it.

When it finally ended, Queen Scelestus was exhausted, but so was her husband. He went to bed without checking on his beloved daughter for once, and he slept in late, complaining of a hangover.

He might not have noticed Lily's absence until the evening if her nursemaid Nancilla hadn't insisted on telling the King that the Princess's bedroom was empty. The nursemaid was the only remainder from Cass's reign as Queen of the house, and she cared too much for her charge. Scelestus had tried firing her on several occasions, but the King kept asserting that Lily was too young.

Still, Scelestus knew she should be grateful for the time she had. Based on Valefor's directives, Lux had to have Lily out of the King's range by now. Really, anything on the other side of the Necrosilvam was beyond his grasp anymore.

Scelestus no longer shared a bed chamber with her husband and hadn't since their first year of marriage. A maid had nervously come into Scelestus's room, telling her of the events, and she had thrown on her dressing gown and rushed to the King's chambers.

After she smeared her make up first to look like she had been crying, of course.

Her husband had already torn his room apart when she arrived, as if stripping the linens from his four-post bed would bring his daughter back. He spent the entire morning ranting and dispatching men to search for Lily and trying to contact anyone who had been at the ball. Nobody remembered seeing the Princess at all, but nobody could seem to remember anything except the spectacular dancing.

Queen Scelestus had to turn away and hide her proud smirk when he'd told her that. Last night, when Lux pushed across the dancefloor, making a scene in his pursuit of Lily, she'd worried that someone would take notice. But no one had, and her enchantments had been quite effective.

The King had sent the last of his men away to scour Insontia for the Princess, and that left he and his wife alone in his bed chamber. Scelestus realized sourly that she'd have to comfort him. He sat on the edge of his bed, in his silk robe tattered around the edges. His gray hair stood up in manic tufts, and he looked older than ever before.

She stood by a window, staring out at the fog rolling in and trying to make herself appear as sad and concerned as the situation called for.

"Did I do something?" he asked wearily.

"Whatever do you mean, darling?" Her voice sounded syrupy, and she hoped it had just the right amount of distress as she went over to join him.

"All I ever wanted was to keep her safe. Did I do something bad to be cursed like this?" He stared up at her with red-rimmed eyes. "First my wife, then my daughter. Why is everyone I care about taken from me?"

"You still have me, Adriel." Scelestus smiled thinly at him and placed her hand over his.

He didn't pull it away, but he hadn't visited her chambers in months. Their marriage hadn't been a sham from the start, at least not on his part, but her spells and enchantments eventually wore off. She wasn't all powerful. Yet.

"I am glad for that." He squeezed her hand once, then let go and folded his hands on his lap.

"Besides, I'm sure Lily wasn't 'taken' from you." She had to look away again, finding it too difficult to suppress her smile. Everything she had ever wanted was about to come true, thanks to that dreadful child.

"What do you mean?" King Adriel asked.

She put her back to him, walking slowly around the room. Worried pacing allowed her to more easily hide her smirks and smiles.

"I've said it before. 'Taken' sounds so *dramatic*, but you've always had a flair for that." Scelestus waved her hands, belittling his fears. "Lily is of an age now where she wants to explore the world for herself. She can't live in this palace forever." Every time she said the word *palace*, it left a bitter taste in her mouth. As if this crumbling shell could even laughingly be referred to as a palace anymore.

"Why not?" the King asked indignantly. "I never moved out of here."

"Of course not, My King, but you are a man." She smiled at him, the way one might smile at a small, incompetent child. "This is your land that you were destined to rule. You had no need to leave."

"Lily is going to rule here," he argued. "I have no other heirs. This is *her* kingdom."

"No, her husband will rule," she corrected him. "For a woman to have any power, she must have a husband." The truth of that struck too close to home, and for once, her face held legitimate sadness. "Lily hasn't had any suitors yet."

"She's never shown any interest!" Adriel blustered, defending his daughter's innocence.

"Not to you. Not to her father," Scelestus said. "And I may not be her mother, but I see things. She confides in me. She knows what society requires of a Princess, and she also knows what her heart yearns for."

He scowled, and his eyes were wide with horror. "You think she left to find a *boy*?"

"I'm merely saying that she hasn't found anyone here." She gestured around them. "Perhaps she thought it best if she explores her options elsewhere."

"I would've found her a suitor, if I had known she wanted for one," he said, sounding defeated.

"I know, darling." Scelestus walked over and rubbed his back. "You're a good father. But she's young, impetuous. She needs to make her own way in the world."

"I hope you're right," he said.

"When will you learn, Adriel?" Scelestus asked. "I always am."

He acquiesced easier than anticipated. Scelestus had been trying to banish that little brat to boarding school for years, but she'd had to settle for locking the Princess away in her room. The King felt safer with his daughter under the same roof as him, and when he'd been unwilling to budge, Scelestus had decided to lean into it. She helped convince him that Lily would only be safe in near total isolation, hidden away, forgotten.

But now Lily was eighteen, and Scelestus wouldn't be able to hide her away for much longer.

She'd marry soon, and eventually, she'd come for her birthright.

And Queen Scelestus couldn't have that.

A small knock came at his chamber doors, and King Adriel summoned the visitor in.

"Excuse me, My King," Jinn said, sliding into the room. He never opened doors very wide, and Scelestus wasn't sure whether it was out of habit from being sneaky, or if he wasn't strong enough to push them all the way. "I don't mean to disturb you in your time of need."

"No, it's quite all right." Adriel had already settled back down on the bed.

"I need to speak with the Queen for a moment." Jinn looked at her.

"*Now?*" Scelestus kept her voice even, but she glared at him.

"It's of grave importance," Jinn persisted, much to her annoyance.

"Is it about my daughter?" Adriel asked.

"No, no." Jinn answered too quickly, and Scelestus was already moving away from Adriel before her servant might say too much.

"Excuse us, My King, I'll be right back." Scelestus hurried out the chambers, and as soon as the door shut behind her, she hissed at Jinn, "What is it?"

"Not here." Jinn eyed the area around them. "The walls have ears."

The servants were notorious for eavesdropping, especially on Scelestus. Any gossip about her was worth her weight in gold, it seemed. She rushed Jinn along as fast as he could go and practically shoved him into a secret passageway. Once she was certain they were safe, she crossed her arms and glared down at him.

41

"Well?"

"I am very sorry." Jinn bowed his head and wrung his hands together. Whatever news he had, he was too afraid to even look at her when he delivered it. "I've just received word from Valefor."

"That my package has arrived on time, in one piece?" Scelestus asked through gritted teeth.

"No, My Queen, I am very sorry," he repeated, his voice growing quiet. "She never arrived. Valefor doesn't know where she – or the delivery boy – might be."

"You mean that arrogant henchman Lux has run off with her?" She seethed and struggled to keep from raising her voice.

"I'm not sure, My Queen." He shook his head. "Valefor did not know, and I have not had a moment to investigate myself. I came to you immediately, as per your wishes."

"Valefor doesn't know where his errand boy is?" Scelestus sneered. "Maybe he's not as powerful as I thought, if he can't keep tabs on one stupid boy and one even stupider girl." She rubbed a hand on her temple and exhaled. "No matter. I'll find them myself. And when I do, I'll slaughter them both."

"Would you like me to get your grimoira?" Jinn asked.

"No. I'll use my cauldron to find Lily. All I need is a lock of her hair. Go fetch her brush from her chambers."

CHAPTER EIGHT

EVER SINCE HE'D MET LILY, nothing had gone right for Lux. When he'd left her in the Necrosilvam last night, he'd been intent on finding a replacement for Valefor and returning to his normal life.

So he set out to find someone. In a bustling tavern in the kingdom north of the woods, he'd flashed his most charming smile at a gorgeous young woman. But when she smiled back, all he could think about was Lily.

The way she smiled up at him. The way she kissed him with reckless abandon. The way she'd curled his hair around her finger.

And the way she'd looked so forlorn and helpless when he'd left her in the cursed forest wearing his oversized jacket.

Lux approached four different women, but it all went the same. His charms fizzled, his words fumbled, and the thought of taking anyone to bed that wasn't Lily was so damn unappealing.

His Master hadn't tried contacting him yet, or at least not as far as Lux knew. He had been avoiding his usual haunts, including his home. He couldn't talk to Valefor yet, not until he had something better to give him than a flimsy excuse.

The night was long and exhausting, and he'd rented a room so he could wash up and get some rest. But sleep never really came. He tossed and turned, unable to get comfortable or shake the feeling of dread.

His solution to this was his solution to so many of life's problems: find someone warm to help him pass the time. Lux didn't even care about finding a replacement for Valefor anymore. He wanted something to calm his nerves, to take the edge off the way he felt.

At the border of the kingdom of Voracitas, buried in a cave on the side of the cliff, was a dank little bar called the Greasy Goblin Tavern. The lights were dim, the patrons were angry, and it smelled of wet dog, so it was not the kind of place that Lux frequented. That made it perfect for avoiding Valefor, but that's not why he went. On any given night, at any given time, he could find Gula seated there, getting sloshed on sweet mead and eating barbecued goblin wings.

Lux didn't really have friends. His lifestyle didn't allow for that, but Gula was the closest thing he had to one. He'd known him the longest, since they'd joined Valefor around the same time, and Gula had to be the friendliest of the peccati. In fact, out of all of them, only Lux and Gula seemed interested in interaction on any level. The rest were happier doing their business and keeping to themselves as much as possible.

When Lux pushed open the door to the bar, a hunchback with one arm tried to trip him. Lux nimbly stepped over him and looked for Gula. He had a booth near the back under a broken lantern that flickered just above his head. Most of the patrons were impish men and goblins who worked in the mines, and Gula stood out like a sore thumb.

Gula was a massive man, with a thick, soft belly and brawny arms, and he stood well over eight feet tall. Lux had never seen Gula come or go, so he could never understand exactly how he fit into the booth. His dark hair hung just past his shoulders, and his green eyes were always smiling. He carried his large frame well, so he was plump and attractive in his own right.

Thick red barbecue sauce coated goblin wings overflowed on the platter before him, and their brittle bones littered the floor where Gula – and the dozens of other patrons in the bar – discarded them. Gula picked up the amber pitcher of mead, drinking from it as if it were a mug, but he lowered it as Lux approached.

"How are the wings tonight?" Lux asked as he slid into the booth across from him.

"Lux, my good man!" Gula's face spread into a happy grin. "I didn't see you come in!"

"I'm keeping a low profile." Lux looked away and motioned for the bartender to bring him a drink.

"Well, that's probably good about now." Gula had a smudge of barbecue sauce on his chin, and he wiped it away as he appraised him.

Lux slipped off his ring and bobbed it back and forth over his knuckles. It was his oldest piece of jewelry, made from shimmering irin bone, and it never wore down or faded, no matter how many times he played with it when he was anxious. He did it now to busy himself, to distract from his fear of Valefor and thoughts of Lily. "What do you mean?"

"You know." Gula glanced around and lowered his voice, then leaned across the table. "Our boss."

"What are you talking about?" Lux looked at him sharply.

"You don't know what you didn't do?" Gula asked dubiously.

45

The bartender dropped a pitcher and a mug on the table with a loud clank, and Lux kept his eyes fixed on the peccati.

"What did you do last night?" Gula asked, just above a whisper.

"Nothing much," Lux said, playing dumb to find out what Gula knew. He had no intention of telling anyone about Lily, or what he'd done with her.

"Did you do the job last night?" Gula asked.

"I picked up a package," Lux replied evasively and poured himself a glass of mead. The mug was still dirty, so he wiped at the rim with his sleeve before taking a drink. "Why? What did you hear? How do you even know about it?"

"How do you think?" Gula gave him a hard look and bit into another wing.

"I don't know what you do or how you find out what's going on," Lux admitted. "I mean this as inoffensively as possible, but I've never understood the point of you. As far as I can tell, you just go around, eating and drinking the tastiest things you can find."

"I do whatever the Master asks of me, but that *is* the point of me," Gula said. "We're all supposed to do our part, and luckily for me, my part makes me very happy. Your part has always been seduction, which is why they suspect you have a hand in this."

"What are you talking about?" Lux asked.

"Last night, were you sent to pick up a girl?"

Lux took another drink of his mead. "I was."

"That girl never arrived at her appointed destination," Gula said seriously. "And I don't want to know where she is or what happened. The Master wants me to find out and report back to him, but he won't come out here to speak to me, so …" He shrugged.

"Can't he just get someone else?" Lux asked. "There's nothing special about this girl."

That was certainly a lie. He couldn't stop thinking of her, and he'd disobeyed Valefor for the first time in his long tenure of service, for *her*.

"I don't know." Gula shook his head. "He wants this one, but he isn't saying why. She's very valuable to him." He lowered his voice even more, afraid of who might be overhearing. "You need to bring him that girl."

"What if I can't?" Lux asked.

Gula's eyes widened with shock. "Did you kill her?"

"No, you know I've never been fond of murder. It's far too messy." He stared off at an empty point on the wall. "I … I *can't* give her to him." He sighed heavily, unsure of how to explain it. "For one thing, I don't have her. But even if I did … she has me completely enchanted. I can't stop thinking about her, and I can't let him hurt her."

"You know what your problem is?" Gula asked. "You're too pretty. You've always been too pretty, and you get everything you want. You can't always get it, Lux. You can have *nearly* everything, but you can't have the things that belong to our Master."

Lux bristled. "She's not a thing, and she doesn't belong to him."

"I don't understand what's going on with you. But he will kill you," Gula insisted. "I'm telling you this as a friend. You need to bring him the girl before he destroys you. I like you, and I don't want to learn to deal with some new jerk because you let someone dazzle you."

47

"I can't do it," Lux said finally. "I don't care what he does to me. I can't bring her to him."

He'd done everything he could to avoid Valefor's wrath all these years, and he wanted to still. But when he thought of his Master hurting Lily, pain blossomed in his chest, and anger burned through him.

Almost anything in the world he'd rather endure than giving her over to him.

"You care more about her than you do yourself?" Gula asked skeptically.

"It appears that way." Lux grimaced and rubbed his temple.

"You're freaking me out a little bit," Gula said.

"It's freaking me out," Lux muttered and took another drink of his mead. "So what am I to expect from him? Total and utter destruction?"

"I shouldn't be telling you this," Gula said.

Lux cocked his head at him. "Telling me what?"

"He's going after the girl." Gula rested his burly arms on the table. "He's not concerned with you, at least not right now."

"What do you mean he's going after the girl?" Lux sat up straighter and looked directly at him. "He's personally going to find her?"

"No, not yet. You know how he hates to leave his lair. He thinks it leaves him vulnerable to attack. But he went right to the big dogs," Gula said. "He sent the canu after her, and he sent Ira."

"*Ira*?" Lux asked in horror. "I've got to go." He stood up. "Thanks for your help."

"Where are you going?" Gula called after him.

"I can't let Ira find her. You know what he'll do to her." Lux shook his head and ran out the door.

The canu were bad enough, but Lux had expected them. He only hoped that the Necrosilvam had

48

enough dark magic to interfere with them. Ira, on the other hand, had a temper far worse than Valefor's. Even if their Master commanded Ira to bring Lily to him alive, if she upset him, Ira wouldn't be able to stop himself from hurting or even killing her.

He hopped on Velox and urged the stallion to race on through the countryside. Lux had won the horse in a card game years ago, with his previous owner alleging that Velox was the fastest horse in all of Cormundie. Lux had never been certain about that, but Velox had proven to be a quick and faithful animal.

Today was no different. He told Velox to go fast, and the horse didn't let him down. But even with Velox's effort, it was still sundown by the time they reached the Necrosilvam, meaning he would have to go in after dark. He didn't care about the creatures in there since they could do little to harm him. That was why he'd left his jacket with Lily – his scent would ward off most anything that lived in the cursed forest. But the darkness would make it harder to find her.

Before going in after her, Lux stopped and stroked his horse's head. "The Necrosilvam is no place for you, Velox. And you don't need to be involved with the canu or Ira either. Go, find a nice pasture, and I will find you when this is all over," he promised him.

This wasn't the first time he'd had to part with Velox. Valefor's errands were often unsafe for a mortal horse, even a fast one. But this was the first time that Lux worried he might not be able to keep up on his promise to find him again. He unbridled the horse and gave him one final pat before bidding him goodbye.

Then he turned and headed into the trees on foot. He cursed himself for leaving Lily alone like that. What had he been thinking? The Necrosilvam was no place for a sheltered Princess.

Lily was clearly special, and his Master would stop at nothing to possess her.

CHAPTER NINE

THROUGHOUT THE DAY, as Lily helped gather things
from the forest, Wick would remark that she ought to
take Lily back to the palace. But for as much as she
threatened it, the witch never did. She'd just mumble
it under her breath while Lily gathered toadstools, and
that would be that.

Lily's gown was filthy from her time in the forest
running from the charuns and the cursed trees, and a
sparkling ballgown wasn't very well-suited for
cottage chores. So Wick had lent her a lovely blue
dress, along with a pair of tattered cloth shoes. The
fabric was faded and fit snug across the chest and
hips, but Lily was grateful for Wick's kindness.

Once she had changed, they had gone out to
forage. Wick needed things for her potions and
enchantments, and she needed food for them to eat.
Sometimes it was hard to tell the difference, but Lily
trusted the witch knew what she was doing.

"It's time to head back to the cottage," Wick
announced as the day grew late. Through the thick
tree branches, Lily could see the sky redden with the
setting sun.

She was crouched down, gathering dead
butterflies from a fallen log as Wick had instructed.
The forest had felt much less foreboding in the
warmth of the day with the witch by her side, but now

she heard the groaning of the trees and the far-off flapping of wings.

"Are we safe out here?" Lily asked.

Wick carried a basket under her arm filled with the treasures from their day's work. Her cloak was draped over her shoulders, but she left the hood down today so Lily could see her face. She walked on, winding through the forest, and Lily hurried to catch up with her.

"I can handle anything in these woods, but I'd rather not," Wick replied. "Which is to say, we're safe, but hurry up."

Lily quickened her pace to keep up with Wick's long strides, and they soon reached the clearing around the cottage. Close to the witch's home, the air seemed warmer and quieter.

"Nothing bothers you here," Lily realized.

"Nothing but lost princesses." Wick looked back over her shoulder, giving Lily a teasing smile.

The apple tree Lily noticed outside the cottage last night was the only living tree she'd seen, with bright blue blossoms and full fruit. Wick had already opened the door and gone inside the cottage, but Lily paused outside to admire the peculiar fruit tree.

The narrow trunk and branches were twisted and wound about, like thread in a rope, and the bark was nearly black. The viridescent leaves were shaped like tear drops and shimmered against the barren scenery of the Necrosilvam. But the most unusual part were the fruits themselves, all of them a startling shade of violet.

"Are these really apples?" Lily reached up and touched one gingerly.

"Of sorts, yes." Wick set the basket down on the dining table and slipped off her cloak. Then she

52

turned to watch Lily through the open door. "Come inside."

"Can I eat one?" Lily asked.

"It won't hurt you, if that's what you're asking." Wick moved about the kitchen, putting everything away. She added crushed butterfly wings to jars or filled up pouches with herbs, making sure everything was in its proper place.

Lily picked an apple from a low branch and took a bite. It tasted bitter and sweet, like vinegar and honey. She wrinkled her nose and went into the cottage, dutifully closing the door behind her. "They don't taste very good."

"They're not supposed to taste like anything. They're not really for eating." Wick wiped her hands on the front of her smock as Lily mulled over the fruit. "They're what keep the charuns and trees from bothering me and my cottage."

"They're magic apples?" Lily asked.

"In a way." Wick gave a small laugh. "I put a spell on the seeds, and everywhere the roots touch, the creatures will never come near. It's not a very strong spell, but it's good enough for what lives around here."

Lily set the apple on the table, not sure what to make of it. It tasted horrible, but it was beautiful and magical, so it seemed like a waste to toss it aside. "Do you need help with anything?"

"No." Wick glanced over at the apple. "You're probably hungry, aren't you?"

"I am quite famished," Lily admitted. They hadn't eaten anything all day, but she hadn't wanted to impose any further on her host by asking.

Food was one of the few pleasures she had in her sheltered life at the palace. Her nursemaid Nancilla brought her meals and delicious pastries. Lily had spent most of her afternoons on the window seat, a book in her lap as she stared out at the lush world beyond her reach. She'd munch on cookies and biscuits, sharing with her pet mice Polly and Poppy, and imagining herself escaping into one of the fables she loved to read.

Wick rummaged through the cupboards and found an old loaf of bread, and she whipped up a simple broth. She served it with a handful of red berries that they'd picked that day, and it was a rather presentable supper.

Lily sat on a stool by the fire, dipping her stale bread into the broth to soften it, while Wick sat at the table. The witch picked absently at her berries and pulled out her grimoira and began writing in it as she ate.

"What are you doing?" Lily asked between bites.

"I'm cataloging everything we collected in my spellbook," she explained. "I like to keep a careful record of everything, because I'm always trying to improve or discover new recipes."

"You're so dedicated to preserving your peaceful life out here. I must be such an intrusion for you. Thank you for taking me in. I really appreciate all of your hospitality," Lily said. Wick mumbled something but didn't look up. "I know my mother would be very grateful to you for this."

At the mention of her mother, Wick stopped writing. She stared down at the page for a moment, and Lily worried that she'd said something wrong.

The witch lifted her head, and her gaze set upon Lux's jacket hanging on the chair across from her.

"Where did you get that?" Wick asked.

Lily swallowed down a chunk of bread to buy herself time. "What?"

"The jacket." Wick set down her pen and faced her, and Lily lowered her head. "Who gave it to you?"

"A … friend," Lily answered finally.

She stopped eating her bread and resorted to tearing it into small bits to busy her hands. The harsh tone in Wick's voice made Lily afraid to say anything about Lux. Not that she even knew what she wanted to say about him at all.

"Whoever gave you this jacket is nobody's friend," Wick told her firmly.

Lily's mind went back to Lux, the way it always seemed to whenever it had a chance. He'd looked at her when he first spied her at the top of the staircase. His eyes had widened, and his lips parted, and it was as if he'd never seen anything more beautiful. He looked at her as if she were the loveliest person he'd ever seen, and her heart sank when she realized that he'd never look upon her again.

CHAPTER TEN

"LILY!" WICK SNAPPED, pulling her out of her thoughts. She'd been staring off into space, daydreaming of Lux, but the witch wasn't ready to move on. "How did you come by this? Did he … did he do something to you?"

Lily shook her head. "No, no, it's nothing like that."

Wick stared expectantly at her, and she knew that the witch wouldn't let up until she gave an explanation.

"I met him at a ball," Lily said at length. "He …" She trailed off, unwilling to tarnish her few memories of Lux with Wick's obvious disapproval. "We talked. He made me feel … *seen*. He asked me to leave with him, and he took me to the Necrosilvam. He told me to go in the woods and hide out, and he made me promise not to go home for three days."

Wick's scowl deepened. "He just left you here?"

"He said I'd be safer here than anywhere else, and that my… *er*, that someone in the palace wanted me dead," Lily faltered, deciding it would be better not to accuse her stepmother of anything just yet.

"When is he coming back for you?" Wick asked.

"He… he isn't," Lily said, and it hurt admitting that aloud.

Lux had left her and told her he'd never see her again. Whenever she remembered their kiss, she never

let herself think about how their time together had
already been spent.

In her heart, she truly believed he'd done what he
had to protect her. But it was over now, and all she
had was a jacket hanging on a chair in a witch's
cottage.

"You think he *rescued* you?" Wick asked, and she
sounded skeptical, bordering on accusatory.

"Yes. I believe he did."

"That is preposterous." Wick shook her head.
"I'm not sure it's even possible. They're incapable of
altruistic actions."

"*They*?" Lily stood up, setting her bowl aside
before walking over to Wick. "What do you know
about him? Who do you think he is?"

"I don't know anything about him personally,"
Wick deflected, and she lowered her head and picked
up her pen, like she meant to just go back to writing
in her grimoira.

"But you know something," Lily persisted.
"Wick, please." She pulled the chair out and sat down
across from her.

"His jacket smells of brimstone." Sighing, she set
her pen inside her book and pushed it aside. "Did
your mother ever tell you about irins and daemons?"

Lily shook her head. "My mother never talked
about anything like that when she was alive. The only
things I know I overheard from the servants talking."

"They're not always reliable sources." Wick
tucked a stray strand of hair behind her ear. "I
suppose Cass planned on waiting until you were old
enough to explain all of this, but she died before she
had the chance. I can't fault her for that, but she's left
you so unprepared."

"Unprepared for what?" Lily asked.

"Our world." Wick smiled thinly at her. "Before the lands of Cormundie belonged to humans, Good and Evil lived openly, locked in a battle with each other. Their immortality made them weary of the same fights, so they devised a wager to settle it forever. Whoever won would have complete reign over the lands, and whoever lost would be banished for all of eternity."

"Are you saying they created humans to settle a bet?" Lily raised a questioning eyebrow.

Wick nodded. "So the story goes. The most cunning daemons were chosen on the side of evil, and the most valiant irins were chosen on the side of good. They were granted powers and privileges to help them, and while one of them was immortality, it came at a price. They had to make sacrifices to stay alive. For the irins, that meant a chaste life, free of many worldly pleasures, but for daemons, that meant something far more deviant."

"What do you mean?" Lily rested her arms on the table, leaning in closer to Wick. "What exactly is an irin or daemon?"

"They're ethereal guardians meant to watch over Cormundie, to help humanity in the pursuit of good. Daemons are practitioners of evil, trying to harm humanity every chance they get.

"Each side also has a leader, one irin and one daemon more powerful than their terrestrial brethren," Wick continued. "These leaders are allowed seven minions to help them on their conquests. While the minions were essentially created equal, so each side would be evenly matched, they had one difference: daemon minions were turned from humans, but irin minions were born."

"So the irin minions are children of angels?" Lily asked.

"Originally, yes." Wick nodded. "In order for them to be pure of heart, they had to be descended from an irin. Luminelle, the leader of the irins, had seven offspring, called virtus. The virtus are here to serve her and help her in her quest to save Cormundie."

"Are the virtus immortal, too?"

"Yes, and no," Wick said. "They can give up their divinity if they choose, rescinding their immortality and servitude for a human life, but to do so, they must bear a child to take their place."

"Why? Why can't Luminelle conceive more children?" Lily asked.

"After her seven children were born, she was struck barren," Wick explained. "That is her sacrifice. She can't have any more children, and there must be seven virtus on Cormundie at all times."

"Why seven?" Lily shook her head, unable to understand.

"Each of the seven represents a virtue: Castimonia, Industria, Moderatio, Humilitas, Pazentia, Caritas, and Gratia," Wick said. "Their names are in the language of old, but they mean Chastity, Diligence, Temperance, Humility, Patience, Charity, and Gratitude."

"They don't have real names?" Lily asked.

"No. When you are under the service of an irin or even a daemon, you don't have your own name or even an identity. Your only wants and needs are that of your Master. Your purpose in life is singular: serve and spread the meaning of your title," Wick said.

"If you are Patience, what do you do? Go around and wait for things?" Lily asked.

"No, you try to *teach* patience," Wick said. "You give people the opportunity to be calm and help them through their strife. While your strength is your own virtue, your mission above all is to help people stay good and true."

"And for every irin there is a daemon counterpart?" Lily asked. "Does that mean for every virtu there is an opposite daemon minion?"

"Yes, unfortunately it does, although they are not offspring of a daemon the way virtus are offspring of Luminelle," Wick said. "Evil doesn't need to be pure to work effectively. Daemons wish only to corrupt, so their minions are humans who have given their allegiance to them. They choose to serve the daemons in exchange for immortality, but like the virtus, it can be given up or taken away."

"I don't understand any of this." Lily shook her head again and leaned back in her seat. "The concept of angels and devils and their servants running about the world. All for what?"

"For the world itself. They have two sides, evenly matched in every way, to see whether Good or Evil will conquer mankind," Wick said. "At the end of time, humans will stand and be counted, their allegiance tallied, their sins weighed against their merits."

"What does this all have to do with me?" Lily asked. She realized that there had to be a reason Wick had brought all this up.

Before the witch could answer, Lily felt a tremor in the air, almost imperceptible. She might have ignored it completely if the apple hadn't begun to move. The violet apple that she had taken a bite out of sat discarded on the dining table, and it started spinning, rapidly gaining momentum.

"What's going on?" she asked.

"*Shh!*" Wick held up her hand to silence her, and the apple abruptly stopped.

CHAPTER ELEVEN

"YOU NEED TO GO," Wick said in a hushed voice.

On the sill outside the window, Wick could barely see the fingers and the face of a small man pressed against the mottled glass. The apple tree wasn't able to ward off anything stronger than a charun, so whoever got through had to be worse.

"What? What's happening?" Lily's skin blanched even further, but Wick didn't have time to explain.

"For your safety, you need to get out now." Wick stood up. Lily got to her feet more slowly, looking confused and afraid, and Wick draped her cloak around Lily's shoulders, and tied it around her neck. "This has some magical properties, not a lot, but it should be enough to protect you through the night."

"Why do I need to go?" Lily looked at her with wide, frightened eyes. She appeared so young, and so much like her mother. Wick touched Lily's cheek with her hand in a rare moment of sentimentality, but then she caught herself and dropped it.

"A long time ago, I promised your mother I'd watch over you, and so far, I've done a poor job of it. This is my chance to make amends." Wick smiled wanly at her and went over to the window on the other side of the cottage, opposite where she'd spotted someone spying on them. "Now hurry, while I still have a chance to do some good."

"Where shall I go?" Lily bustled up the length of her dress as she got ready to escape.

"You need to be resourceful," Wick said as she boosted her out of the window. Lily hung onto the frame and dropped to the ground. "I'll come for you if I can. But if I don't, keep moving. Run as fast and as far as you can."

"Thank you," Lily whispered and pulled the hood up over her head and darted across the clearing.

Her feet made no sound as they padded along the mossy earth, and she ran into the trees of the Necrosilvam, into uncertain darkness.

Wick grabbed her wand, a gnarled, twisting piece of bronze — the horn of a deceased unicorn. Many things around the cottage could be used to create some very powerful potions, but she didn't have the time to make them.

She rummaged through the vials on the shelves. Most of them were innocuous things like sleep aids and wound healers, and she knocked a blue vial of plant growth serum to the ground. It shattered, liquid splattering everywhere, and almost instantly, a small white flower grew from between the floorboards.

"Impressive. For a novice witch." Scelestus's voice echoed through the small space, and Wick whirled around to see her standing in the middle of the cottage, with an iridescent dark blue gown flaring around her. Without a sound or a puff of smoke, the sorceress had appeared in Wick's home. "But you're not a novice witch, are you?"

Wick had seen her before. In the wedding, only a short time into the dark months that followed after Cass's death. The widowed king had married very quickly, to the exuberant peacock of a sorceress who had just crashed into her home.

During the wedding, Wick hadn't paid her much mind since her attention had mainly been on the toddler Princess. Her nursemaid had been so devoted and caring. Cass had sworn that the nursemaid loved Lily as much as she did.

The King had moved on, and Lily was in good hands, so Wick had slunk off to her cottage. She'd thought everyone would be better off that way.

But now, as she realized that Lily was running for her life from her own stepmother, Wick knew she'd made a terrible mistake.

"I'm not as practiced as I once was." Wick straightened her shoulders and gripped her wand more tightly. "But don't be fooled by my appearance. I know a few things about magic."

"Yes, I can imagine," she said. Wick raised her wand at Scelestus, but it was only enough to make the sorceress laugh. "There's no need for that, at least not yet. I'm looking for someone who belongs to me, and as soon as you return her, I can be out of your hair. No harm done."

"There's no one else here," Wick said.

"I'm sure that's true." Scelestus glanced derisively around the cottage. "There isn't enough room here to hide anything. But you must know where she is."

"I don't know what you're talking about, and I can't help you," Wick told her evenly.

"Now listen here, you pitiful witch, I want what is *mine*." Scelestus swirled her hand in front of her, waggling her fingers until a ball of fire appeared in the palm of her hand. "I will burn this place down, running every last bit of this little haven you've made for yourself, if you don't tell me where the girl is."

"I don't know where she is," Wick insisted. "And if you burn this down, I'll destroy you."

"Destroy *me*?" Scelestus threw back her head and cackled, and the sound sent chills down Wick's spine. It was a laugh she'd heard before when Cass was still alive.

"You're that horrible old woman!" Wick's hand trembled with rage. "Your clothes are nicer, your make up is better, but you're still that haggard woman underneath it all!"

It had been a week before Cass died that they had met her, but then she'd been a beggar woman, practicing her sorcery in dirty rags in dark alleys. Wick had been travelling with Queen Cass, strolling through the town. Scelestus had done a simple trick for her, and Cass had been so pleased, she paid her with a ruby.

Scelestus had laughed, a wicked sound darkening one of the last happy memories Wick had with Cass. And then the Queen had fallen ill and died within a few days' time.

"Is that when you decided?" Wick asked Scelestus. "That very day you performed a trick, is that when you decided that it wasn't enough to want Cass's life, you had to take it for yourself?"

Scelestus smiled wider. "You're Cass's friend?"

"Yes." Wick gritted her teeth. Already, she was drawing her energy up, calling everything she had. "You took advantage of her innocence and her charity. But I am not nearly as kind or forgiving as she would have been."

"You couldn't stop me from killing her, and you can't stop me from killing her daughter." The fire ball in her hand burned brighter, and Scelestus raised her hand.

Before she had a chance to throw it, Wick's wand glowed blue and shimmered. A beam of light flashed out of it, enveloping Scelestus, freezing her in place. She struggled against it, her mouth contorting in rage and pain, but Wick was using all her might to hold her.

"*Invictus evictum!*" Wick shouted and flicked the wand.

Scelestus went flying through the window, shattering glass and splintering wood. Her body slammed hard against a tree several yards from the cottage, and she slumped down on the ground.

Wick had used all of her energy to cast Scelestus out of her cottage. She had wanted to kill her, but she needed to rest and recharge.

As it was, she had to drag herself to her grimoira on the table. Her muscles were weak, and her mind had gone hazy. Even her vision blurred, making it hard to see the words on the pages. If only she hadn't grown stale and complacent these past fifteen years. Most of her practice went into potions and holistic cures these days.

And then she heard the howling. To the untrained, it sounded like maniacal wolves – a howl mixed with a mad man's laughter. But Wick knew it was the calling card of the canu.

The canu were a pack of hybrid daemon dogs, and they worked for Valefor, the powerful daemon. Scelestus would be the least of Wick's worries if Valefor had gotten involved.

Too late, she realized the canu were howling in delight, the way they did when they caught their prey.

"*Lily.*"

CHAPTER TWELVE

LILY RAN THROUGH THE FOREST, Wick's cloak
billowing behind her. All around her, she heard the
forest groaning and yearning, and the branches
scraped against the cloak and tangled in her long hair.
The moon was bright and full, but trees closed in,
blotting out its precious light. She could hardly see
beyond the end of her nose, and she narrowly missed
running smack into a tree several times.

The angry flap of charun wings echoed through
the forest. She didn't know where she was going or
what she would do when she got there, but she had to
keep running. Wick had stayed back to protect her,
and Lily wouldn't let that be in vain.

When she heard a booming sound coming from
the cottage, that was the only time she stopped.
Dazzling blue light spiraled up through the treetops,
and Lily watched in awe until it disappeared.

Then she heard something new.

Lily had grown accustomed to the sounds of the
animals that scurried about the forest floor. She rarely
saw them, but she knew their grumbles and padded
footsteps, and this was something else entirely.

The density of the trees made it hard to tell what
they were, or even how many, but it sounded like a lot
to her. Even their breathing was angry, broken up by
growling or gnashing teeth.

She soon realized that they weren't breathing
heavy – they were *sniffing*, searching for something.

Her heart pounded in her chest, and her hair stood up on the back of her neck.

The air smelled faintly of burning, like the scent after a flame had been extinguished. If she could smell *them*, that meant that they could likely smell her.

One of the beasts howled, a strange resonation mixed with an excited screech. She could hear charuns flapping their wings, dispersing into the night as the heavy footfalls raced past them. Even they were frightened away.

Lily turned and ran for her life.

Her legs moved as quickly as they could, churning underneath her, but she knew it wasn't fast enough. The beasts hunting her howled again, and they sounded much closer than they had before. In the shadows, she sensed a rabid pack of movement.

She darted through a narrow gap between the trees, and she nearly ran straight into a beast. Her feet skidded on the muddy ground, stopping mere inches from the growling muzzle. The trees parted enough for the moon to break through, and the light glinted off the massive incisors in the beast's jaws.

The animal vaguely resembled a dog, but much larger, standing almost as tall as Lily when they were still on all fours. The skin was like charred leather and hairless. Her first thought was of Old Tom, the farm cat that moused at the palace. He had been burned in a barn fire years ago, and his puckered scarring was nearly identical to this beast's.

But this was something much angrier and more dangerous than Old Tom. They had paws the size of her head. For a moment, though, before the beast bared their jagged teeth at her, she wondered, *Is this truly a monster, or is this another tortured animal?*

irtue

She felt hot breath blowing on her cloak. Another one of the dogs was behind her, and four others had surrounded her.

"Stay calm." She held up her hands palm out, moving in a slow circle so she could keep her eyes on all of them. "Please, I won't do you any harm." One of the beasts growled and stepped toward her. "Stop!"

She wrapped the cloak more tightly around her, hoping that its magic could ward them off. The beast kept walking forward, and Lily had no choice but to step back. The one behind her moved to the side so she could get by. All six moved together, walking as a pack in front of her as she walked backwards.

They were herding her along.

They snarled and growled as saliva dripped from their teeth. Their muscles trembled with restraint as they sniffed and huffed at her.

Lily decided that her only chance of survival was to run for it. She doubted she was as fast as they were, but she was much smaller. If she darted and weaved through the trees, she might be able to lose them.

So, she bolted. She'd barely made it four steps when a giant paw slammed into her back, knocking her to the ground.

Claws tore the cloak and ripped into her soft flesh. She would've screamed, but the beast stood on her back and her face was pressed into the mud. She breathed dirt, and she couldn't even cough it up.

Her lungs burned as she retched into the ground. Finally, the weight lessened on her body. She lifted her head up, gasping for air between violent coughs. A paw still pressed against her, holding her in place, but with less control than the beast had before.

The scratches on her back felt on fire, and she screamed. Not for help or mercy, but simply because

71

she couldn't stop herself. Her veins were burning, sending a searing pain through her entire body. The beast must have had venom in their claws, filling her with poison.

Her mind went hazy, her thoughts turning black and blurry. A gust of wind blew over her, and using all her remaining strength, she craned her neck back, and she was surprised to find the beast gone. Pain blotted out most of her other senses, but her fear gave her some clarity. She struggled to sit up and saw one of the beasts fly into a tree, as if they had been thrown.

Lux stood in front of the dogs, squaring off with them and holding a giant stick in his hand. One of the animals charged and hurled themself at Lux, but he raised the stick and impaled the beast in the side.

The animal yelped and then fell to the ground. They lay a few feet away from Lily, twitching and whimpering, and even through her fiery pain, she felt sorry for the pitiful creature.

The others snarled and snapped at Lux. He held his hand up, his palm facing them, and the beasts all began to whine, as if in pain. One of them yelped, then turned tail and started running away, and the rest quickly followed.

The one Lux had impaled struggled to get to their feet, whining. Lux walked over to it, and the animal cowered before him. He grabbed the stick and yanked it out, making the dog howl in pain. Using his hand, he signaled them to leave. The dog got to their feet, then hobbled away.

Lux was suddenly at Lily's side, and he wiped the mud from her face. Her skin burned everywhere, but she leaned into his caress, finding comfort in his touch even in the most terrible of moments. Her vision was fading, and her strength was seeping from her body.

"I worried I'd never see you again," she said through labored breaths.

"I'm so sorry that I left you," he said.

The last thing she saw was his handsome face, his strong features tight with regret, and she heard the panic in his voice as he yelled, "Lily, stay with me! *Lily*!"

And then the darkness consumed her.

CHAPTER THIRTEEN

LUX HAD HOPED he'd gotten to her soon enough, before the canu could harm her, but when Lily went limp in his arms, he knew he was much too late.

His arm cradled underneath her was wet – he'd thought from mud – but now he pulled it back and saw the red of her blood and the faint green glimmer of canu venom.

"Damned dogs," he cursed, but he had no time to waste. Still holding her in his arms, he got to his feet and carried her to the creek.

On his way to tracking Lily and the canu through the Necrosilvam, he'd passed a brook, and that would be his best option to help her. Clean the wound to get out as much venom as possible, burn it to destroy the rest, and pack it with cool blue moss to ease the pain. It was a rather simple treatment, but she would be in agony until it was done. Once she lost consciousness, she'd be consumed by pain.

She mumbled something into his chest, and Lux ran faster, chasing the distant sound of the brook.

"We're almost there," he told her.

The water shimmered, reflecting the moon in the night. He skidded down the embankment, moving carefully so Lily wouldn't be hurt further. On the soft mud and reeds beside the brook, he gingerly laid her on her stomach. He took off her cloak and tore open the back of her dress to access her wounds. The venom glowed in the thick gashes, cut diagonally down her back until her hip.

Lux cupped his hands, filling them with ice-cold water before spilling it onto her back. She twitched and moaned, and he worked quickly. Using the edge of the cloak and the water, he scrubbed at the wounds, and Lily screamed.

He offered apologies, but he doubted she heard him over her cries. When he was certain he'd got out as much as he could, he ran his fingers down her gashes. Flames licked out from the tips of his fingers, and the air smelled of burning flesh as he seared and cauterized her wounds.

With the venom, the canu assault, and the fiery treatment, she had to be in incredible pain. Lily had stopped screaming, but she sobbed loudly, her whole body shaking from the intensity of it.

Lux scrambled to his feet and looked around, hoping that blue moss was nearby. It thrived on water and death, and this area of the Necrosilvam was full of both. Lily lay on her stomach with the back of her dress torn open, and he didn't want to leave her vulnerable like that, but he couldn't ignore her pain either.

He jogged a short way down the brook, still close enough to see her, and thankfully, he found blue moss growing on the underside of a log.

"This will be over soon," Lux promised Lily when he returned to her. He knelt on the ground and smeared her wounds with the moss.

Almost instantly, he felt her skin cool beneath his hands, and she stopped crying. Lily sat up slowly and wiped at her tears. Lux wrapped her cloak around her, covering her exposed back, and shielding her from the cold.

"Thank you," Lily said.

"It was nothing." Lux sat next to her on the embankment.

She stared down at the water and pulled the cloak more tightly around her. "What are you doing out here?"

"I came for you," he said honestly.

"Why?" she asked.

"Because I never should've left you in the first place," he said, his voice low and husky. "I'm so sorry for what you must have endured."

"How did you find me?" Lily asked, daring to look at him from the corners of her eyes.

"The canu."

He tracked the canu using another one of his peccati tricks. A benefit of his position was the ability to call on the daemon dogs, and he could psychically link with them. When he did he saw what they saw, but so could any of the other peccati or even Valefor, if they chose that moment to check in with this pack. Any one of them may have witnessed him intervening to save Lily.

They ought to start moving, but she looked exhausted. She required rest, and he'd worry about Valefor after that. For now, what she needed was time, so that's what he'd give her.

"What are the canu?"

"Daemon dogs," Lux said.

"How did you chase them away?" Lily asked.

"Magic." He smiled at her, hoping to distract her from realizing he hadn't really answered the question.

He didn't want to explain them to her, how they were in the service of his Master, and even Lux himself. The canu tracked and hunted anything the peccati or Valefor wanted, and the canu protected them from their enemies.

To further distract her, he asked, "How are you feeling?"

"Much, much better. Thank you." She looked up at him with big doe eyes, and Lux could see the depth of her admiration in them, a reverence he knew he didn't deserve. "You saved my life."

He couldn't handle the way she gazed at him, the way she made his heart race, and he lowered his eyes. "I only saved you a bit of pain. Canu venom isn't deadly – it's just excruciating."

"Thank you all the same, Lux," she said.

She knelt down at the brook's edge, splashing cold water on her face to clean herself up.

"Do you feel well enough to walk?" Lux asked once she'd finished washing.

She nodded. "I think so."

Lux stood first and took her hand to help her. As soon as she touched him, that wonderful feeling rolled through him. Her skin always felt so cool against his warm hands. A strand of hair stuck to her damp cheek, and he brushed it back, letting his hand linger there.

He wanted to kiss her more than anything, but he was afraid if he started, he'd never stop.

"We should get going." He dropped his hand from her cheek and backed away from her. He still held her hand so he could help her up the embankment, but he had to put some distance between the two of them.

She slipped a few times climbing, and Lux initially blamed it on the muddy incline. But when she got to the top, she collapsed, falling heavily into his arms.

"Sorry," she whispered, leaning against him. Her hair smelled of flowers and fresh spring water, and Lux held her in his arms for a moment before steadying her.

The moon sat high in the sky, so it was still several hours before dawn. He'd bought them some time by chasing the canu off. It'd be a few hours before the dogs made it back to Valefor, and then he'd have to mount a counterattack. Lux should use the time to get a head start, but Lily was too weak.

"Come on." Lux kept his arm around her waist and led her over to a massive tree. "You need to get some sleep before we can continue."

"Are you sure that's safe?"

"I won't let anything happen to you," he promised her, and he meant it.

"I know," she said simply.

The roots of the tree sprung out of the ground, creating a perfect little nook. He took off Lily's cloak and spread it over the ground like a blanket. He slipped off his jacket, then sat down on the cloak, leaning back against the trunk of the tree. Lily rested her head on his chest and draped her arm over his waist. He took his jacket and covered her up with it. When he wrapped his arm around her, she nestled into him.

In that moment, Lux felt complete for the first time. He hadn't even realized anything was missing until he met her, but now, with her curled up in his arms, her hair tickling against his chin, he couldn't imagine being without her.

Within moments, Lily fell asleep, comfortable in the safety of his embrace. He stayed awake for much longer, keeping watch for danger and appreciating every second with her.

CHAPTER FOURTEEN

HIS NECK HURT from the way he'd been sleeping, and he stretched out his arms. It wasn't until he felt the empty space beside him that he realized something was missing. Lux opened his eyes to the morning sun, and she was gone.

"Lily?" He looked around, his heart racing when he saw no sign of her, and he jumped to his feet. "*Lily!*"

He raked a hand through his hair and feared the worst. He never should've slept. He shouldn't have closed his eyes, even for a moment. Lily needed him to protect her, and he'd failed again.

"Lily!" Lux shouted into the Necrosilvam.

"I'm right here," she said, her voice like a melody of a familiar song.

Her head appeared over the embankment as she climbed up it. As soon as he saw her, he wanted to run to her, but, as not to alarm her, he settled for a brisk walk. She wore his jacket, the sleeves rolled up to keep them from drowning her hands. Her long, dark hair was tied up in a loose braid, with small white flowers woven through it.

"I went to collect berries for breakfast." Lily used the front of her dress as a pouch, overflowing with red berries. "I picked these yesterday with Wick, and they're a bit tart, but they're safe to eat."

She'd been smiling down at her berry haul, but when she looked up at him, her expression faltered.

81

She put a hand on his chest, her palm flat above his heart, and her eyes widened. "Your heart is racing, and you look so frightened. Did something happen?"

He put his hand over hers and offered her a crooked smile. "No. For a moment, I was afraid I lost you."

"I never meant to give you a fright. I only wanted to show my gratitude for your help by gathering a nice breakfast."

"Then we should eat and enjoy your bounty."

Lux moved away from her then, because he wouldn't be able to resist kissing her for much longer. When she looked up at him, with her dark eyes full of yearning and hope, all he wanted to do was pull her into his arms and lose himself in her.

But now wasn't the time or the place. Lily was recovering from her injuries, and they were at the edge of the Necrosilvam. His Master would send more daemon dogs and other minions after them, and Lux had no idea where he could take Lily that Valefor couldn't reach eventually.

He'd need to do something to conceal them if he had any hope of keeping her hidden from Valefor, but he had to gather a few supplies for that.

"Why don't you get breakfast set up?" Lux suggested, and he motioned to where her cloak was spread out in the crook of the tree. "I need to clean up first."

"Of course. Take all the time you need."

He watched her for a moment, over his shoulder. Lily was humming to herself as she set up a picnic, and he had to hope she'd be safe for a few minutes out of his eyesight. He went down the embankment to the brook, and he immediately started scouring the area for something like a fish or rat.

For the concealing hex, he needed blood. The Necrosilvam didn't have much in the way of benign wildlife, but he managed to find a recently dead bullfrog.

"Sorry, little guy, but you'll have to do," he muttered.

Using his finger, he tore open the underbelly so he could drip the blood into the palm of his hand. He recited an incantation he'd learned long ago, and he smeared some of the animal's blood on his inner wrists. Lily would need the same thing done to her, but it would be simple enough when he held her hands.

It wasn't an all-powerful concealing hex, and truthfully, Lux had only dabbled in sorcery when he first started serving Valefor. But it would work for a day before he needed to redo it, and if they kept a low profile, they *might* be safe.

When he returned to Lily, she was still humming. She smiled brightly at him as he sat down across from her.

"These are quite delicious," he said, once he'd tried the berries. They were bitter with a touch of sweetness, but he hadn't eaten since the Greasy Goblin Tavern, so he was happy for anything to fill his stomach. "You said you found these with Wick before? Who is Wick?"

"She's… she's my friend," Lily answered. She sounded uncertain, but she nodded, as if to confirm it to herself. "She's a witch who lives in a cottage in the woods, and she helped me after you left." Her expression darkened.

The berries soured in his belly, and he hoped that someday she could forgive him for leaving her.

"We need to go back for Wick," Lily said, looking back at the cursed wood. "She sent me away last night, before the canu came. They may have hurt her. We should go back and make sure she's safe."

"If the canu found her..." He shook his head. "We can't go back. And if she's a witch, she can protect herself."

Lily frowned, her worried eyes still on the trees. "Wick seemed capable... but I wish I knew that she was all right." She turned back to him. "Are you a witch, like her?"

He laughed and nearly choked on a berry. "No. I'm nothing like that."

"Then what are you?" she asked.

He avoided her curious gaze and ran a hand through his hair. "I'm just a man who wants to make sure you're safe."

"Why? Why do you care if I live or die?"

He exhaled roughly and tried to find the words to explain how he felt for her. And the shame that he'd even considered handing her over to his Master.

"It's my fault that you're in this mess because I'm the one who brought you to the Necrosilvam," he said finally. "And when you kissed me in the palace..." He trailed off and licked his lips, and he braved meeting her eyes. "I want to be someone worthy of kissing you again."

"What if I told you that you already are?" she asked.

His fist clenched, crushing the berries in his palm, and he used all his restraint to keep from pulling her into his arms right then.

"I would tell you that you don't know me very well." He cleared his throat, and then because he needed to do something before his self-control broke,

84

he stood up. "We should get moving. We need to put distance between us and where the canu found you."

CHAPTER FIFTEEN

"WHERE ARE WE GOING?" Lily asked.

He picked up the cloak they'd been using as a blanket. He shook off the twigs and dirt, then did a trade with her – she wore the cloak, while he put on his own jacket.

"I don't have anywhere that I know is safe," he admitted as they started walking. "In a few days, when the canu have moved on, I will take you back to Insontia. But until then, we need to keep going."

"How did the canu know to come after me?" Lily asked. "My stepmother is a sorceress, but I've never known her to use anything like a canu. At least not that I have ever seen."

"She has a friend who can control them," he said, but that was taking liberties with the word "friend." Valefor had none, and even if he did, he'd never consider a dreadful sorceress like Queen Scelestus a friend.

"Who?" Lily pressed.

"A daemon," he said flatly, because he didn't want to talk about Valefor or how he served him. To keep her from pursuing those questions, Lux asked, "How are you feeling? You were attacked badly last night and slept in tree roots. Are you able to walk okay?"

"I'm walking, so I am well enough," she said, but she was moving rather slow.

She limped subtly, and she took his hand when she needed to step over a thick root. Afterward, she didn't let go, and honestly he preferred it that way. Walking beside her, her hand enveloped in his.

But if she were to find out what he really was, she'd be repulsed by him forever.

They walked most of the morning saying very little. Lux would've loved to talk with her, but he was afraid of the questions she'd ask. The Necrosilvam seemed to stretch on forever, but soon they'd be reaching the edge of it, and they wouldn't have its dark magic to help cloak them.

A log had fallen across their path, and Lux helped Lily over it. His thoughts were on his cloaking hex and wondering if it would last until nightfall, and not on the log. The rotted wood gave out under her foot. He caught her just before she fell to the ground, and he held her in his arms for a second before setting her on her feet.

He took her hand, preparing to lead her forward, but she stopped. A mewing sound, similar to a kitten or a frightened rabbit, came from the log. She pulled away from him and went back to peer inside the fragmented wood.

"Oh my!" Lily gasped.

Lux looked over her shoulder. A giant furball surrounded by three smaller furballs had made a modest nest inside the rotten log. They were almost perfectly round and covered in plush, golden fur with small round ears, a tuft of a tail, and comically large eyes. Their feet were hidden entirely under their fluff, pressed close to their chubby bellies.

"It's a mama and her babies," Lily said.

"Those are auratus."

The fluffy mother tried to stand in front of her babies, but they kept running around her, mewing. Lily reached in and scooped up a baby in her hands, while the mother chirped loudly at her.

"What are you doing?" Lux asked as Lily sat down on the sturdier part of the log, cradling the baby auratus in her hand.

"Making sure they're all right." Lily carefully petted and inspected the baby. "I have a pair of pet field mice at home called Polly and Poppy. These little auratus remind me of them."

"How do they seem?" he asked.

"Good so far." She put that one back in the log and picked up another. This one sat timidly in her hand, not moving as much as the first one, and the auratus didn't seem to be mewing at all. She pet the back, hoping to illicit some kind of response, but the baby just sat quietly in her hand. "Oh no. I think something's wrong with this one."

Lux considered telling her to put the auratus baby back, let nature take its course, so they could get on their way, but when he saw her face, he couldn't. She was already heartbroken over her part in upsetting the fluffy little ball.

He crouched down in front of her. "Let me see." He held out his hand, and gingerly, she passed the tiny baby to him.

Lux had no tricks for this. What little power he had had never been used for healing, or good of any kind. He only hoped that he could coax the little guy into feeling better. He pet the baby gently, and within a few moments, the fluff ball started rubbing against his hand and purring.

"You saved him!" Lily sounded in awe.

"He was just in shock, that's all." He smiled, handing the auratus back to her.

"But how do you do the things you do?" she asked him.

"I don't know what you mean." He straightened up, putting space between himself and her question.

"The canu last night, you chased them away." The auratus ran around her lap, and she played with the baby absently. "Without even touching them."

"I used a big stick, remember?" Lux shifted uncomfortably and stepped away from her.

"No, you did something. You communicated with them." She switched out the auratus on her lap for the last one, to make sure they were all okay. The baby licked her hand, and satisfied that they were all fine, Lily turned her full attention on him.

"What are you, Lux?" she asked, letting the baby run about her lap. "You made the canu leave. Those awful charun bird-goblins never come out when you're around, and the trees don't reach out for you like they do me. Nothing comes out or bothers you."

"Oh, plenty of things bother me," he muttered.

"Your jacket smells of brimstone," she said.

"You … you can smell that?"

"No." She shook her head and set the auratus back in the log, reuniting the little family, and then she stood up. "It's too faint for me. But Wick noticed the scent, and she told me not to trust you."

"But you do," he said, because he could see it in her eyes. She wore her heart on her sleeve.

"I do." She took a step to him. "But should I?"

"Yes," he said simply. "If the auratus are safe, we should move on."

CHAPTER SIXTEEN

QUEEN SCELESTUS SOAKED IN A TUB filled with warm water and a healing tonic that smelled of lavender. Her body yet ached from her encounter with that old cottage witch last night, and the bath provided some respite.

It had been far too long since Scelestus had battled anyone, and Jinn had barely gotten her home afterward. She considered going back to finish off the witch, but it wasn't worth the risk. In a few days, when she successfully recaptured Lily, she would have more than enough power to do away with the witch, and anyone else who crossed her.

But for now, she was old, tired, and painfully mortal. Her time was best spent back in her chambers, using the cauldron to track down Lily. Once she got done recuperating in her bath, of course.

"Do you need anything more, My Queen?" Jinn asked. He'd been hobbling around the room, lighting candles, pouring her drinks, and disturbing her peace.

"No, Jinn, you've done enough," she replied wearily and took a sip of her ignis brandy.

"I wanted to be sure, Mistress," he said in his sniveling way. "You were assaulted with magic and nearly died."

"I did not *nearly* die!" Queen Scelestus seethed at him over her steaming water. "The old hag surprised me and threw me into a tree. It was little more than a sucker punch."

"Yes, of course, My Queen," Jinn said hurriedly. "I didn't mean to imply you are weak enough to be killed by someone inferior to you."

"Of course not," she muttered.

But the harsh truth was that Jinn wasn't entirely wrong. Scelestus had underestimated the cottage witch because she was unkempt and alone, which was a bitter twist of irony. That's exactly what Queen Scelestus had been when she met the witch all those years ago.

Back then, she had been just Scelestus, no Queen, no title, no riches, no home. She'd once been an advisor to a king, and before that, the consort of a duke, and before that, she served a prince. Eventually, their wives or their children had grown suspicious of the beautiful sorceress.

To their credit, she had been conning the men out of as much gold and jewels as she could with her charms and her magic. Although, it was never more than what she deserved. But it always ended the same, with the royal family tossing her penniless into the street. Without money for her supplies, her magic weakened, and her true age showed.

That was when she met Casteline, Queen of Insontia, and her witch friend. They'd been walking hand-in-hand, smiling, and whispering in each other's ears.

All that Scelestus could see was their jewels, their youth, and their beauty... and they're unadulterated happiness. She wanted Cass's life, and she vowed that it would all be hers. She worked tirelessly to get all she needed, and soon enough, Scelestus procured a poisoned apple.

She handed it to Queen Cass in the market with a toothy grin. Cass had smiled and thanked her.

A week later, Cass was dead. Six months after that, Scelestus was the Queen of Insontia. The Queen is dead. Long live the Queen.

She finally had her title, with wealth to her name, and when her husband and stepdaughter died, everything would belong to her. Not just the palace but the entire kingdom. She would claim it for her own.

With Lily on the cusp of her own monarchy, Scelestus had to get rid of her. She'd ventured outside of her usual channels for such a delicate job, and Valefor was a powerful daemon. She'd stupidly trusted that he could make things happen, and he had even offered her something far better than Insontia.

It was supposed to be a simple exchange but it had all gone afoul thanks to Valefor's stupid errand boy. Now she had to find the girl herself, and she'd have to kill that cottage witch as soon as she had her strength back.

"Are you sure you don't need anything from me, My Queen?" Jinn asked again, and he lingered beside her tub.

She waved him off. "Yes, yes, be gone with you already."

"Thank you, Mistress." He bowed and headed toward the door, but he paused and looked back at her. "Was that you, Mistress?"

"What are you babbling about?" she snapped, but then she heard it, too.

Bubbling from her cauldron on the far side of the room, followed by a booming voice saying, "*Scelestus.*"

"It's Valefor," she realized.

She was exhausted, nursing embarrassing injuries, and she wore no makeup, or even clothes. It

93

was perhaps the worst possible time for the daemon to call on her. She certainly didn't want him to see her this way, but she could never turn down a chance to see Valefor.

"What should we do?" Jinn asked her.

"Get me my robe and help me out of this bath, you nitwit!" Queen Scelestus shouted at him. "I must answer when he calls upon me!"

Jinn ran to fetch her satin robe, but he still didn't move fast enough. She yelled at him again and cursed under her breath.

"Queen Scelestus," the daemon's voice boomed from the cauldron again, and finally she was out of the bath and wrapped in her robe.

"Lord Valefor, I'm here," she said as she hurried over to her cauldron. The dark water bubbled up at her, but she could not see his face in its murky depths. He was denying her the privilege of looking at his face, and she scowled.

"My name is Valefor," he corrected her, sounding annoyed. "'Lord' is a title humans give themselves to feel important, so it's not something that I need or desire."

She grimaced. "Of course, Valefor. I am sorry."

"I don't need your apologies," he growled. "I need to know where my princess is."

"I tracked her to the Necrosilvam," she said. "But she had a witch helping her and –"

"Is the witch the one who sent my canu away?" he interrupted.

"I did not see any canu," she answered truthfully, but she did not remember much of the immediate aftermath of her confrontation with the cottage witch.

"They were howling in the cursed wood," Jinn interjected, and she glared down at him, even though his utterance had been helpful.

"A witch cannot command the canu," Scelestus said. "That is something only a daemon can do."

"Not only daemons," Valefor said, and she remembered that it extended to his minions.

"You think your boy is helping her?" she asked with a grim smile. If it was Valefor's mistake, he might owe her something more for her trouble than what they had agreed upon.

"He's not my boy. He is my *servant*," the daemon snarled. "If he is involved, I will find him, and I will destroy him. But you needn't concern yourself with that. You only need worry about getting me what is mine."

"I don't have the Princess –"

"Then find her!" Valefor shouted, and his voice shook through the chambers. "Send out your kingdom's men. Search your lands high and low."

"Yes, of course," she agreed quickly. "She's a scared, stupid girl. She can't have gone far."

"Good," the daemon said. "The next time we speak, I expect to have the Princess in my possession."

The cauldron stopped bubbling, and his voice had gone silent. The conversation was over.

"What do we do now, Mistress?" Jinn asked.

She had found Lily last time by using a lock of hair and the cauldron, but when she had tried it again earlier today, she hadn't been able to find anything. Something was concealing Lily's whereabouts from her, but no matter. She had other magic at her disposal.

"We find that damned brat and the idiot boy whose helping her," Scelestus said with a wicked smile.

CHAPTER SEVENTEEN

THEY MADE IT TO THE EDGE of the Necrosilvam by afternoon, and Lily realized something. She stood with the dark cursed forest behind her, and a rolling golden wheat field of the Goldlands before her. The fields belonged the kingdom of Zelus, the realm to the northeast of Insontia, but Lily had only read about them and seen pictures of the lush fields painted in her books.

"Is something the matter?" Lux asked. He was a step in front of her, still holding her hand as he faced her.

"No," she said with a nervous smile. "This is the farthest I've ever been from home."

"Really?" He arched a dubious eyebrow. "Weren't you invited to royal parties all over the lands?"

"I imagine that we were, but I was never permitted to attend," she said with a weary sigh. "My mother was killed when I was young, and my father became overprotective. I was never allowed out of Insontia. He thought he could keep me safe that way."

He studied her a moment, a thoughtful expression on his face, and he smiled softly. "Well, Lily –" He tilted his head. "What is your full name?"

"Liliana Casteline Adriella," she said.

Lux bowed slightly before her and announced, "Liliana Casteline Adriella, welcome to the rest of the world." He straightened and gestured expansively to the rolling fields around them.

She laughed. "Thank you. I don't think I've ever had a warmer welcome."

With that, she stepped further than she ever had before, and she walked with Lux through the fields.

"So, if your father is so overprotective, how did he end up married to a woman who wants you dead?" Lux asked.

"I'm not sure actually. I've been trying to make sense of it myself."

Outside of the forest, with the terrain smoother, Lux tried to pick up the pace, but Lily couldn't quite match it. One of the claw marks on her back ran down to her hip, and every step she took caused an ache to flare all down her left leg.

She tried to keep up, but he noticed her struggle, even though she attempted to hide it, and he slowed to match her.

"My father loved my mother very much. Too much, maybe," Lily explained to keep her mind off the pain. "He was madly, completely in love with her, and when she died, he fell into an awful despair. I didn't see him for months, and he hardly left his room.

"But eventually he came out, and he met Scelestus, and she was the first thing that made him smile since my mother," Lily went on. "She was good for him, but she never liked me. Father didn't notice it because he wanted me safe, with a nursemaid always by my side, and Scelestus wanted me out of the way. They both got what they wanted when I was locked in my room."

"And what did *you* want?" he asked gently.

"I…" She floundered for an answer because she couldn't remember the last time anyone asked her that. "I wanted to play in the sun, and I wanted to dance in the moonlight, and I wanted to love someone."

Then she realized what she'd said, and her cheeks burned with shame as she lowered her eyes. It sounded so silly and presumptuous, but that was the deepest wish she had in her heart. She had so much love she wanted to share, but all she had been left with were the thin pages of her fairy tales and a couple of tiny field mice.

"Well, we're out in the sun," Lux said. "And we danced in the moonlight outside of your palace." He smiled down at her. "Two out of three is a very good start."

"It certainly is," she agreed. "What about you?"

"What about me?" he countered with a laugh.

"What was your life like before we met?"

"It's hard to remember all those days ago."

"Come now, Lux. I've told you so much about myself, and yet I know next to nothing about you."

He sighed and relented. "My life is not terribly interesting. I was born a nobleman's son who raised me to be a nobleman, but I have never been all that noble."

"You've been nothing but noble with me," she assured him, and he laughed again, but it rang hollow.

"Maybe you bring the nobility out of me," he said.

"Have you killed many people?"

He looked sharply at her, his eyes wide with surprise. "*What*?"

"Aren't you a sellsword?" Lily asked. "Didn't Queen Scelestus hire you to kill me?"

"Oh." He lowered his head, letting his blond hair fall across his forehead. "Well."

"Well, what?" she pressed. "What does that mean?"

"I was never supposed to kill you. I was to kidnap you and bring you to the man I work for." He spoke slowly, picking his words carefully, and he only took fleeting glances at her. "I was chosen because I'm charming, and they thought you would leave with me."

"What does the man you work for want with me?" she asked.

"I'm not sure, honestly. But I know that it can't be any good."

They walked in silence for a while after that, with Lily processing all he'd said. Everyone kept telling her not to trust Lux – even he'd told her that before – but she had heard the fear in his voice when he couldn't find her this morning, and she'd felt his arms around her all night long while she slept.

"It looks like there's an old mill up ahead." Lux pointed to a building on the horizon. "We should set up camp for the night when we reach it."

"But there's so much day left," she protested.

"You need to rest, and you need to eat," he said firmly. "I know you've been trying to hide how much pain you're in, but I see you wincing when you step."

"I don't want to slow us down."

"We're hurrying to keep you safe. I can't protect you to the detriment of you." He shook his head. "I may be new to being a guardian but even I know that doesn't make sense."

"We still have a ways to go until we reach the mill," Lily said. "That gives you plenty of time to tell me something real about you."

"Something real?" he echoed.

"Something true, something that matters."

His forehead scrunched, and he frowned as he thought. Finally, he said, "I only have one friend."

"Really?" she asked, taken aback. He was handsome and charming, so she imagined that he had dozens of friends.

"His name is Gula," Lux said. "He's the only one that really knows me, knows all that I am, and he would still fight by my side if I asked him to."

"Well, now you have *two* friends," she responded cheerily.

He shook his head. "You don't really know me."

"Lux." She stopped, but she still held his hand, so he turned back to her. "Someday, if you show me who you truly are, I promise you I will still be your friend."

He smiled then, but his eyes were pained. "I hope so."

CHAPTER EIGHTEEN

WHILE LUX HAD BEEN OUT gathering food and firewood, Lily stayed behind and tidied up the abandoned old mill. He hadn't been gone that long – he didn't feel safe leaving her alone – but she'd managed to make the place much more comfortable in that short time.

Lily had swept cobwebs and set up a makeshift sitting area out of straw and her cloak. When he came in, she was sweeping and humming to herself.

"You didn't need to do all this," he told her.

"I wanted us to have somewhere nice where we could spend the night," she said with a shrug.

The back of her dress was torn open, and she'd tried to stitch it up with loose ribbons pulled from the bodice, but the fabric was gapping. He could still see her wounds, red and angry as they slowly healed.

He put down the wood he'd gathered, and his pockets were overflowing with mushrooms and herbs he found growing outside.

"Lily, sit and rest." He gently took her arm and led her over to her improvised sofa.

"You don't need to tend to me because I am a princess," she demurred.

"I'm tending to you because you're hurt, and I want you to get better. You've walked a lot today, and we still have much further to go."

"Thank you for being so kind to me," she said. His hand was still on her elbow, and she put her hand on his as she smiled up at him.

"If I were kind, I wouldn't have gone to that ball at all," he told her honestly. A kind man didn't scheme to kidnap young women, or so many of the other things he'd done in his life.

"Still, I am glad that you did, because otherwise I may never have met you." Her eyes were so wide and bright when she said that, and he knew that she meant it.

"Me too," he said softly. It was so hard not to kiss her when she looked at him like that.

He cleared his throat and pulled away. "I should start the fire and make us something to eat. You must be starving."

Later, after they'd eaten a hearty meal of mushrooms and tubers, Lux and Lily sat on the cloak by the small fire in the hearth. The mill walls were cracked in places, and the lone window had no glass in the panes. As the sun set, the air grew cooler, and fireflies came out to dance across the fields.

"The fireflies are out," he said.

His attention was on the shimmering bugs, but from the corner of his eye, he saw Lily slide up next to him. When she rested her head on his shoulder, his breath caught in his throat. It was such a simple gesture, but he suddenly had butterflies in his stomach like he had when he was a boy.

Tentatively, he put an arm around her, and she leaned deeper into him.

"They are so wonderful," she murmured, sounding awed. "I've never seen them so close. From high in the tower where my bedroom is, they're nothing but specks of light, like far-off stars. But now I see they're more like little fairies."

"At least they don't bite the way fairies do," he said, and he realized that she was trembling. He tensed and asked, "Is something wrong? You're shaking."

"No, no," she assured him quickly. "I'm just a bit cold."

Of course she was. Her dress left her so exposed, and she wasn't accustomed to sleeping outside. Lux grabbed up the cloak swathing it around them both like a blanket. Then he wrapped his arms around her and pulled her close to him.

"Is that better?" he asked when they were cocooned together.

"Much better." She curled up against him. "You're so warm."

Like all peccati, Lux ran hot, but he didn't explain that to her. Not yet. He rested his cheek on top of her head, and he wanted to enjoy their time together instead of thinking about how doomed this all was.

"When you were in your room, other than watching faraway fireflies, how else did you pass the time?" Lux asked.

"I read all of my books, and then I read them again," she said. "When I got bored of that, I'd make up my own stories. Sometimes, I'd tell my nursemaid Nancilla, but usually I just told them to myself."

"What kind of stories?" he asked.

"All kinds. Princesses rescued by knights, pirates searching for treasure, anything with romance and adventure and a happily ever after."

"Would you tell me one now?" he asked.

"I'd feel silly." She squirmed, and when he looked down, he saw the blush on her cheeks. "And what if you don't like it?"

"I don't want you to do anything that makes you uncomfortable," he assured her. "But I am certain that I would like any story you wanted to share with me."

Lily took a deep breath, and she began:

Once upon a time, in a far-off kingdom, a boy wanted very much to be good. His father was an important man, and the boy worried he would never be all that his father wanted him to be.

So the boy chose a different path, and he found a life of adventure. He traveled the world, seeing amazing sights, and dining on exotic foods. But that life came with a cost.

He served a Master who called on him to do bad things, and the boy did what had to be done. But still, the boy had lines he would not cross, commands he could not obey.

Deep down, the boy never stopped wanting to be good. His Master made his life lonely, and the boy worried that was as he deserved.

But one day, the boy met a girl, and she could see all the good in him that he tried to hide. So, she kissed him, and she was exceptionally happy he'd found her.

"Does this story have a happy ending?" he asked thickly.

She pulled away, so she could look up at him with a soft smile. "I hope so."

"Lily…" he said breathlessly, and his eyes were on her pale pink lips. Longing consumed him. It was a palpable agony resisting the way his body demanded to kiss her, touch her, complete her.

"I… I don't want to hurt you, and I think that you're too good for me, and that you deserve far more than I could ever offer. But if you ask me to kiss you, I won't be able to deny you," he told her in a husky voice, and by then, his body was nearly vibrating with want.

Lily raised her chin defiantly, and he could already see the gleam in her eye. Before she even spoke, he was already pulling her closer, moving his hand carefully up her side.

"Kiss me, Lux," she commanded in a whisper, and then finally, blissfully, he let go.

ℭHAPTER ℕINETEEN

LUX KISSED HER and stole the air from her lungs. She melted against him, into him, and she wrapped her arms around him so she could cling to him.

When her hand went to his neck, pulling him closer, her finger found a curl at the nape. He moaned against her mouth.

His tongue parted her lips, eager and hungry, and the heat of his body chased away any chill that she felt. One of his hands went to her breasts. It was already overflowing over the top of the ill-fitting dress, and with a quick movement, he freed it completely.

His other found the ribbons that barely held her torn dress together, and he made quick work of unfastening them, but his mouth never parted from hers.

Lily wanted to be closer to him still, *needed* it. Since the moment she met him, before she even kissed him, she'd felt an inexorable draw to him. Like a tether between them, pulling them together.

She'd thought it had been between their hearts, but the urge pulling her now came from between her legs. It was an unbridled, desperate desire. She craved him as she craved air and water.

The aches from her injuries had all but evaporated, and she climbed onto his lap, straddling him between her legs. Her dress fell free, pooling around her waist, and his mouth trailed down to her neck as his hands explored her body.

His touch was tender and careful, deftly avoiding the wounds and bruises to find the places on her body that would only bring pleasure. His kisses trailed down her neck, his teeth scraping lightly across her collarbone, and delighted shivers rolled over her.

Her hands were buried in his hair and gripping onto his back. The cloak had fallen away, and the fire warmed her bare skin. She tilted her head back, and she begged, "More."

Lux stopped kissing her to look at her, and his blue eyes burned with yearning. His voice was low and hoarse when he asked, "*More*?"

"I want more of you," she said as she brushed his golden locks from his face. "I need you."

A hungry smile curved on his lips. "Who am I to deny a princess what she needs?"

He let go of her long enough to pull his shirt up over his head, and she allowed herself a moment to take in the sight of his broad shoulders and firm chest.

But then they were kissing again, and his hand slid between her legs. He freed himself first, undoing his pants, and then his hand went to the warmth inside her, and she moaned against him.

Somehow, her body knew what to do. She rocked gently against him, and he put a hand on her waist to help guide her up and down. They moved very slow at first, finding each other and cresting their rhythm.

But the heat was building inside her, growing more insistent, and they quickened together.

All at once, a bliss exploded inside her, a million tiny points of pleasure and happiness dancing all along her skin, and he exhaled roughly as he pulled her close.

Lux laid back on the cloak, pulling her down with him. She lay on top of him, her head on his chest, and both of them caught their breath.

"That was wonderful," she said finally. He laughed, a warm rumbling that shook through her.

"Indeed it was." He kissed the top of her head and stroked her hair. "But… I want you to know this isn't why I came back for you."

She lifted her head to look at him. "Are you saying that you didn't enjoy that?"

"No, no, I *very* much enjoyed being with you," he amended hurriedly. "But I didn't expect it. I even tried to avoid giving into my… my wants."

Her brow furrowed in confusion. "Why were you avoiding *that*?"

Lily had heard of making love before. Some of the fables she read even mentioned young women being swept off their feet by a handsome prince, where he'd take her to their marital bed to make love.

But none of them let on how amazing it would feel. Her whole body still tingled with happiness, and she had never been closer to anyone as she had been with Lux. His heart had beat inside her, he had breathed into her lungs.

After a lifetime of cold loneliness, Lily hadn't even imagined that she could feel the way she did now. Safe, warm, happy, *whole*.

So for Lux to say that he'd been avoiding that sounded like madness to her.

"Well, because you are a Princess, and we are not married," he said finally.

"Neither of those sound like good enough reasons," she argued. "Happiness and love are things that should be shared and celebrated, not avoided or locked away."

"That is very true," he agreed and caressed her face as she leaned into his palm. "But I don't want to hurt you."

She smiled then because it was simple. "Then don't."

The length of the day hit her all at once. She yawned, then shivered as a chill ran over her. Her body still felt like goo, all happy and melted, but the night air was chasing away the earlier heat.

Lily slid off Lux and curled up into his side. He pulled the cloak around her, enveloping her in his arms, and she soon drifted off to sleep.

She didn't know how long she slept, but it was dark and cold when she awoke. Lux tensed beside her, then he pulled away and sat up.

"Lily, get dressed," he commanded. "Something's wrong."

"What is it?" she asked as she hurried to do as he said.

But Lux didn't answer. He fastened his trousers, then grabbed his shirt and stood up. He peered out the mill window. The fireflies were long gone, and Lily realized she could smell the air smoldering.

CHAPTER TWENTY

HE'D WOKEN UP TO THE SCENT OF BRIMSTONE, and a charge in the air. Lux didn't know who was here, but he knew it wouldn't be good.

Lily was dressed, wrapped in a cloak, sitting on the hay, and he stood at her side, wielding a rusted pitchfork. That was the best he could come up with to protect her.

"What is it that you're afraid of?" Lily asked quietly. "All the terrible things in the Necrosilvam were afraid of you."

"Not *all* the terrible things are afraid of him," a voice taunted.

He leaned against the doorframe – he'd somehow opened the mill door without Lux noticing – and he was lit by the moon. It'd been a while since Lux had seen him, and Ira looked bigger than he remembered. He stood a foot taller than Lux, and his broad shoulders were all but busting out the inseams of his suit. His black hair hung just past his shoulders, and he had a hard face, like it'd been made of stone.

But then again, maybe it had. Ira had always been more powerful than Lux, more powerful than everyone, except Valefor.

"How did you find us?" Lux asked.

"I'll admit, it was difficult at first," Ira said. "You somehow managed to do an adequate job of covering your tracks. But I knew you couldn't keep it up forever. I was hunting you in the Necrosilvam, and then I felt your power."

Ira gave him a knowing smirk, and Lux moved in front of Lily, blocking her from Ira's predatory gaze.

Lux cursed himself under his breath. The concealing hex could only protect from so much. When a peccati expressed their truest purpose and desire, a surge rippled through all of them. For Ira, that might mean bashing someone's head in. For Lux, it meant taking someone to bed, the way he just had with Lily.

It was his fault. He hadn't been thinking, and he brought Ira right to them.

Lux winced and clenched his fist around the pitchfork. He would do anything to prevent Ira from hurting Lily, so he swallowed down his anger and fear, and forced a charming grin.

"Ira, I can make you a deal."

"What could you possibly have to offer me?" Ira smiled, revealing long, sharp incisors as he circled closer.

"I've always had things you wanted," Lux said.

Ira wasn't as prone to greed as some of the others, but like all peccati, he had a pull toward the finer things in life. In particular, Ira had often eyed the ring Lux always wore.

The ring was gorgeous. A shimmering pearlescent bit of irin's bone carved by an expert thaumaturgy blacksmith into a stunning ring. Lux had gotten it as a gift from his father, and it was nearly indestructible and completely irreplaceable.

Lux held up his right hand, tapping the ring with his thumb, and he saw Ira's gaze go straight to it.

"I will give you this ring if you leave. All you have to do is walk out of here and pretend you never saw us. Our Master will never know, and you'll have something you've wanted for a very long time."

Ira cocked his eyebrow. "You said you'd never part with that."

"I did," Lux said. "But I will. Now. If you just do nothing."

Ira snorted and shook his head, and Lux's last bit of hope that this would end well had evaporated.

"It's no good," Ira said. "Others will come for you soon, if I don't capture you, and Valefor would skin me alive if he ever discovered I let you slip through my grasp.

"Besides," Ira said with a grin, "Valefor is offering a mighty reward for bringing him the Princess. He wants her now, and he's willing to give almost anything."

"Why?" Lux asked, genuinely exasperated. "Why does he want her?"

"You could ask yourself the same question." Ira nodded to Lily standing behind Lux. "It's cute what you're doing here, and I've always known that you were soft. You've never had the passion for this like I have."

"If by 'this' you mean torture and destruction, then no, I've never had a passion for that," Lux admitted. "But that doesn't mean that I'm not capable of it."

"Are you threatening me, little man?" Ira took another step toward him, his eyes blazing and his fists clenched at his sides. It took very little to set him off, and he'd never liked Lux.

"You can't take her," Lux told him evenly. "I can make a deal with you, but I won't let you leave with her."

"Like you can stop me?" Ira asked with a laugh.

"Lux, please," Lily pleaded. "This doesn't need to come to violence."

"Why don't you listen to the girl?" Ira said. "Sounds like she wants to go with me."

Lux kept his eyes on Lily. He couldn't kiss her goodbye or tell her any of the things he needed to. How sorry he was that he put her in danger, but he'd loved every moment he spent with her. How much he cared for her, and how his heart started beating around her – *for* her – after years of lying dormant.

But instead of any of that, he told her, "Run, Lily. Keep running and never look back."

He shook free of her touch, and he turned on Ira. He blitzed forward with the pitchfork raised, hoping for the element of surprise.

The prongs of the pitchfork landed right in Ira's broad chest, but the metal bent and snapped. The pitchfork gave, but Ira didn't. He just laughed, and then he punched Lux so hard he went flying across the mill.

He slid across the floor, but Lux jumped back up to his feet and charged at him again. Ira caught his arm and bent it backwards. Lux heard it snap, but he wouldn't drop to his knees. He kicked and punched at Ira, but it felt as if he was boxing granite.

"I'd love to finish this hand-to-hand," Ira said finally. "You know I always loved beating you to a bloody pulp. But Valefor is waiting, and I need this to be over."

Blood dripped into Lux's eye as he stared bleakly up at him. Ira held his hand palm out toward him, and Lux remembered too late that Ira always had the better powers.

Red light streamed out of Ira's palm, hitting Lux right in the chest, and instantly, the pain was

everywhere, scorching through him. Lux collapsed to
the floor, only vaguely aware of a world beyond his
agony. His blood literally boiled inside of him, and he
smelled his own searing flesh. He couldn't burn, not
with flames, but this was magic cooking him.

Through it all, he heard Lily screaming. Then
finally, his body gave up, and everything went black.

CHAPTER TWENTY-ONE

BEFORE HE OPENED HIS EYES, he felt the burning in his chest. Lux tried to move, but his arms were weighted down, shackled at his wrists. With excruciating clarity, he remembered the sound of Lily's screams, and he knew Ira had taken Lily.

His eyes flew open, and he struggled to sit up.

"Oy!" a woman snapped. "Settle down, unless you want to hurt yourself worse."

He couldn't sit up completely, thanks to thin strands of silver that lay over his wrists and ankles, but he stopped fighting enough that he could take in his surroundings.

The cottage was tiny, and it looked like it had weathered a small battle recently. Everything was a mess, and part of one wall and the roof were missing. Lux lay pinned in a bed, his shirt removed. His bare chest had a large, dark circle over his heart, the mark left from Ira's magic.

"What's going on?" Lux demanded.

"Why don't you tell me?" The woman stood in front of the damaged wall, a tub of wet clay and a pile of thatched roofing by her feet.

"You're the one that's holding me captive!" Lux growled and pulled at his wrists again, but they refused to budge. "What is this? Why can't I move?"

"It's irin hair." His captor brushed a lock of her hair from her forehead, leaving a muddy trail behind on her skin. Her dress and skin were stained with clay and dirt from the work she was doing. "That particular strand came from Sofiel. Have you been acquainted with her?"

"No, I've never met an irin." Lux lay back on the bed, groaning in frustration. "Can you please let me go? I don't have time to waste."

"You're a peccati, aren't you?" She put her hands on her hips and stared at him. "There's no point in lying. Your reaction to the irin hair confirms it."

"If you know what I am, then why are you asking?" Lux countered wearily.

She stepped closer, inspecting him. "Peccati can't be burned by flames or traditional magic, so the only thing that could've left that kind of mark is one of your own."

"You seem to know a lot about me without telling me a thing about you," Lux said. "And I appreciate your curiosity, but I can't stay here any longer. Someone needs my help."

"Do you mean Lily?" the woman asked.

Lux narrowed his eyes. "What do you know of her? Who are you?"

"I'm a friend of Lily's." She crossed her arms over her chest and returned his suspicious glare. "Wick."

"You're the witch?" Lux asked, remembering when Lily had mentioned her. "Do you know where Lily is?"

"No. I was hoping you would be able to tell me."

He stared up at the ceiling and swallowed back his regret. Lily was either on her way to Valefor's or already there by now. "She was taken by another peccati. I need to go so I can find her."

"How were you injured?" Wick asked.

"Trying to protect her." He looked back to her. "And if you care about her at all, you'll let me go so I can find her."

"You shouldn't go anywhere just yet. You're still healing." Wick reached down and took the irin hair from his wrists. "Don't try anything. I have magic, and you're not well."

Lux sat up, and he really felt the ache in his body for the first time. Peccati healed incredibly fast, but she was right. He wasn't done yet, and his bones cracked when he moved.

"Does Valefor have her?" Wick asked, watching him carefully.

"I don't know. Not yet, I don't think." He cracked his neck, wincing at the pain. "I'm not sure how long I was out, and Ira took her."

"Ira?" Her face paled. "You mean 'wrath?'"

"Yes."

As each virtu exemplified one of the sacred virtues, each peccati was a vice. Quick-tempered, mean, violent, and more powerful than any of the other seven, Ira had one purpose in life: be angry and make everyone else angry.

Of all the peccati that could've taken Lily, Ira had to be the most dangerous.

"Where's my shirt?" Lux looked around the room, eager to get on his way.

"It was destroyed." Wick turned and gestured to his jacket hanging on the chair, the one that he'd given Lily before he left her in the Necrosilvam. "I believe that's your jacket, though."

"Thank you." Lux went over to the chair, his gait more labored than usual.

"Who are you?" Wick asked.

121

"Lux," he replied absently and slipped on his jacket.

"As in Luxuria?" A cynical smile crossed her lips. "*Lust*? I never should've taken the irin hair off of you."

"It doesn't matter what you think of me." Lux tried to ignore her as he fixed the collar of his jacket. "I'm going to help Lily."

"You're not going anywhere near Lily." Wick pulled her wand from her waistband and stepped toward him. "I'm not going to let her be some conquest for you."

He looked away from her and shook her head. "You don't know what you're talking about."

She scoffed. "As if you would pass up the chance for the bragging rights of the millennia! The Luxuria bedding the Castimonia. What a stunning feat that would be."

"What?" His stomach dropped, and it got harder to breathe. "She's the Castimonia? She's ... *chastity*?"

Lily was a virtu. The Castimonia. His exact opposite. He reached out for the chair next to him, and he collapsed into it.

CHAPTER TWENTY-TWO

"WHY WOULDN'T SHE TELL ME?" Lux asked finally when he found his voice.

"I don't think she knows yet." Wick lowered her wand as she studied him. "You really didn't know?"

"No." He shook his head. "She can't be." He exhaled roughly. "What have I done?"

"What *did* you do?" Wick asked him sharply.

"I-I don't know," he insisted.

She sighed in disgust. "You slept with her, didn't you?"

He looked up and swallowed down his guilt. "What … what does that mean for her?"

"Don't you know anything about virtus?"

"Not much," he admitted. "Our lifestyles keep us separate, and I never concerned myself with what any of the others are up to."

"So you're lazy as well as lustful," she muttered, then sat down in the chair across from him. "You didn't destroy her or steal her soul, if that's what you're thinking." Wick lowered her eyes when she clarified, "The Castimonia is allowed to have… relations."

"Chastity can sleep around?" Lux asked dubiously.

In truth, he did know very little about how the virtu worked. To spread the work of the irin, Castimonia couldn't just sit around abstaining from

123

carnal urges. Doing nothing at all was hardly an effective recruitment.

To be any kind of servant, they had to have an action towards good, not simply the absence of evil. But he didn't see how having relations would be on the Castimonia's list of duties.

"The purpose of a virtu is to spread love and kindness above all else," Wick explained. "Chastity is about the integration of spirituality with the physical body in sexual intercourse. It's the union of the divine and the human. Being chaste means not following one's desire with selfish abandon, but desires met with love, kindness, and connection can be pursued."

"How do you know so much about virtus?" Lux glanced around the tiny cottage, overflowing with herbs and crystals. "You appear to be a witch and a hermit, and yet you know more about Lily than she seems to know about herself."

"I knew her mother. *Intimately*. She was the Castimonia before she died," Wick said and leaned back in her chair.

"Was she not married before she died? The King is a widower –"

"I loved Cass," Wick interrupted him. A sprig of lavender sat on the table, and she picked it up, twisting it between her hands. "And she loved me. I didn't meet her until after she was married, after she'd had Lily, but what we shared was pure and kind and sacred."

"You… you're saying the Castimonia had an affair with you?" Lux asked.

That sounded more like something he would do. In fact, a large part of his work had been tempting someone away from their spouse. While Lux always strived for reciprocal pleasure, there was never any love or connection involved, and only sporadic kindness. His role was using his sexuality to pull people away from the good in their life, and of course, taking care of whatever errands that Valefor might send him on.

"Cass married the King of Insontia because he was kind, and she could do good works as his Queen," Wick said. "As ruler, she shifted money from wealthy nobleman's coffers and palace exuberances and diverted it toward the townsfolk and the kingdom."

Lux remembered the Insontian palace had seemed in ill-repair. He'd assumed it was a poor and failing kingdom, since he never spent much time in Insontia, but perhaps he was seeing the long-term effects of Lily's mother, who prioritized her people over a gawdy palace.

"Cass had already lived a very long life when I met her," Wick went on. "She was ready to retire, to pass her work on to her daughter as soon as Lily was old enough. But she never had the chance. Her husband didn't know what she truly was because he wouldn't understand. He's a kind man, but very simple.

"He'd grown up sheltered and privileged in his own right, and he wanted to keep Lily safe, so he locked her up," she said. "As a stranger to him, and a hermit witch, I was never allowed access to Lily. I assumed an irin would find her when the time was right to help guide her as the Castimonia, but ... that hasn't happened." Then she gave him an accusatory glare. "And Lily was safe, until she met you."

Lux flinched, but he shot back, "Her stepmother sold Lily to my Master. I'd hardly call that safe."

"What are you doing?" Wick asked. "You didn't know she was the Castimonia, you're not taking her to your Master, you fought with your brethren over her. You're not capable of love, so what do you want with her?"

He lowered his eyes and ran his fingers through his hair. "I don't know what I'm capable of anymore."

"How do you think this will all end? A *sin* and a *virtue*, living happily ever after? Do you think her Master would allow it? Or yours?" Wick asked, but now her tone was almost gentle.

"She doesn't have a Master yet," he realized. If Lily didn't know that she was the Castimonia, she couldn't have taken the vows to serve anyone.

"Was that the plan? Bring her to your Master so she could serve him instead?"

"No! I don't want her anywhere near him!" Lux shouted, anger rising up at the thought of Valefor with Lily. "If he touches a hair on her head —" He balled his hand up into a fist and gritted his teeth to keep from lashing out at anything around him.

"You really care about her?" Wick asked, studying him.

"Yes," Lux said.

"You can help me rescue Lily," she said finally. "But once she's free, I'll do everything to keep her away from you."

He only nodded because he couldn't blame her. Maybe Lily did need protection from him.

"Lie down and finish resting," Wick told him and went over to her shelves. "I need to get things together before we go, if I'm going to be fighting."

"We really don't have much time. Every moment she's with Valefor …" Lux trailed off, unwilling to finish the thought.

"You need to be as strong as you can be if we're going to go up against Valefor." Wick shot him a look over her shoulder. "He is the most powerful daemon in Cormundie, isn't he?"

Lux grumbled in response and grudgingly went to lay down on her bed. She was right, but he hated doing nothing.

"I don't know why I'm trusting you," Wick said, muttering to herself, as she shoved vials into a small sack. "You're all master manipulators and liars, especially Luxuria."

"I don't know why you speak so harshly of me. We've never met before," Lux said tiredly.

"No, but I know your kind." She opened a vial and tasted a bit of the potion, then recapped it and tossed it in her pouch. "There's a reason I live alone in the woods."

Lux had noticed that Wick was a beautiful woman, despite her attempts to hide it. Before he met Lily, he would've tried a charming smile on Wick, but he doubted it would work. He wondered of the life she must've had that had driven her out here.

He stared up at the hole in the ceiling. "How did that happen?"

"What?" Wick went over to the large wooden chest on the other side of the room, and she glanced up at the carnage done to her cottage. "Oh, that? Just a fight with a sorceress." Something occurred to her, and she stopped rummaging to look back at him. "It was Scelestus, Lily's stepmother. You had business with her, didn't you?"

"Valefor and Scelestus planned some kind of exchange, but I'm not sure of the details. All I know is that he sent me to get Lily from her, but instead of bringing her to him, I left her in the woods."

"Ah, yes. Leaving a young girl alone in the Necrosilvam. What a wise decision," Wick said sarcastically.

"I didn't know what else to do." Lux sighed. "Obviously, I regret it. I should've stayed with her."

"There's nothing to regret. I took care of her then, and I'll take care of her now," Wick said. "She fares much better with me than she does you."

"She's still with Ira, no matter who you blame," Lux countered.

"Not for much longer." She found something in her wood chest and held it out to him. "Here. Put this on."

"What is it?" He sat up as she tossed white cloth at him.

"It's a shirt."

"I thought you said you didn't have a shirt." He slipped off his jacket and pulled on the black tunic. It didn't have buttons, but the collar hung open, the way he liked it.

"No, I said your shirt was destroyed. This one should protect you from magic, so your friend Ira won't scorch you alive if you see him again."

"Well, thank you." He adjusted the shirt, fixing it so it laid right on him. "I know it pains you to help me."

"It really does," she admitted. "But I don't see that I have a choice in the matter."

"Why did you even bring me back here?" He got to his feet, feeling too frustrated to rest any longer. Most of the aches in his body had worn away, and the burning in his chest had disappeared almost entirely. "You hate me so much, and I've never done anything to you."

"I was tracking Lily but I found you instead, and then the trail went cold. I brought you back because you might be my only way to find her," Wick said. "My only love was the last Castimonia, and she spent her whole life trying to spread good and fix the damage you and your brethren did. Now her daughter is involved with you, everything she stood against. Cass would be devastated if she knew what was happening."

"It doesn't matter if her dead mother approves of me or not," Lux said. "It only matters that we find Lily. When this is all done, you can spit in my face, for all I care. But right now, I need you to stop focusing on your hatred of me. I know I can't do this on my own, not after the way Ira took me out, but I doubt you'd fare well against him or Valefor, either. We need each other. For Lily."

"You're right." Wick took a breath. "I know I have another cloak around here. As soon as I find it, we can leave."

Lux went to the hole in her wall, staring out at the night. The moon was still swollen, shining down on the Necrosilvam. When he was around, the woods were silent, but he didn't understand how anyone could live out here. The charuns were troublesome, and the trees were known for thieving. The purple apple tree was lovely, though, but he'd never seen one before. As he admired it, the branches started quivering.

Then he felt a fluctuation, as if the world pulled and swayed. A gust of wind blew through the house, and an apple fell from the tree, landing on the ground with a thud.

Something was coming, and Lux turned just as the front door swung open.

CHAPTER TWENTY-THREE

WICK HAD HER HAND ON HER WAND, and Lux was instantly at her side, his stance defensive.

A tall, lean man strode inside her house as if he was an old friend, but Wick had never seen him before. His clothes were even finer than Lux's, all silks and leather. Gaudy rings ordained both his hands, and a heavy chain hung around his neck. His features were refined and delicate, giving him an aristocratic handsomeness, and wavy chestnut hair landed just below his shoulders. He surveyed the room with contempt, his calculating dark eyes sweeping over everything and dismissing it all within seconds.

"You didn't have to clean up on my account," he said drolly. He ran his finger along the counter and gave a derisive glance toward the hole in her wall.

"Who are you and what do you want?" Wick demanded.

She hadn't raised her wand yet, and she didn't want to waste her energy if she didn't need to. Her encounter with Scelestus had left her down for hours, and she didn't have the time to waste. Her other hand dropped into her pouch, digging for something to frighten her uninvited guest away.

"Ava, what are you doing here?" Lux asked when the man didn't answer.

"Ava?" Wick questioned, looking at Lux out of the corner of her eye. "Avaritia? Greed?"

"Right." Ava smiled at her, flashing perfect white teeth. "It's a good thing you're smart, because your new friend here is a complete fool."

"Why are you here?" Lux asked, ignoring his jabs.

Ava turned his attention to Lux. "I came to see what trouble you'd gotten yourself into."

"What I do doesn't concern you," Lux said flatly. "I don't have anything you want. You have no reason to be here."

"Oh, I know you don't have anything!" Ava gestured to the mess. "I've been hearing all about your terrible fall from grace, as it were, and I had to see it for myself. Disasters are so much better up close."

Lux narrowed his eyes at him. "What have you heard?"

"That you've completely lost your mind. You've betrayed Valefor, and you've been plotting to keep the Castimonia for yourself." He picked absently at his manicured nails.

"You know she's the Castimonia?" Lux sounded shocked, and Wick glanced over at him.

Ava smirked. "Oh my. You're even dumber than I thought. What on Cormundie did you possibly want with that wretched girl?"

"Nothing you would understand," Lux muttered. "Have you come to escort me back to Valefor?"

"No. I've never been much of an errand boy, though I certainly do a better job than you." Ava winked at him. "Valefor is so busy with the girl, he hasn't been able to deal with you yet. But don't worry. He means to destroy you."

"I wouldn't have expected any less of him," Lux said with a resigned sigh.

132

Ava procured an embroidered handkerchief from his pocket and wiped at a spot on the counter. Once he was satisfied it was clean, he leaned back against it.

Wick still gripped the wand in her hand. So far, Lux appeared more annoyed than afraid. Just the same, she wouldn't take chances with a pair of peccati. The cottage smelled too much of brimstone, and Wick sneezed.

"You're allergic to clean then?" Ava asked with an arched eyebrow.

"Are you two old friends?" Wick ignored him and wiped at her nose with her sleeve, making him wrinkle his face in disgust.

"We go way back," Lux said.

"Yes, I suppose we do," Ava mused, picking at his nails again.

"What does Valefor want with Lily?" Lux asked.

"Who?" Ava asked with a feign of innocence.

"*Lily*. The Castimonia," Lux clarified through his jaw clenched.

"Oh. I wasn't aware that she had a name." Avaritia shrugged, and Lux made an irritated growl and glared at him. "Valefor wants her because she is the Castimonia, obviously."

"She's not yet, not really," Wick was quick to amend. "She hasn't taken her vows yet."

"*Precisely!*" Ava pointed at her and beamed. "See! I knew you were smart."

Lux shook his head. "If she's not a true virtu, why does he want her?"

"He wants her to take her vows *to him*," Ava explained as if they were both small children. "If she serves him, a daemon, and not an irin, he's won. *We* have won."

"What?" Lux asked, but Wick's jaw dropped as understanding finally hit her.

"The most epic battle of all time!" Ava motioned abstractly around them, referencing everything. "Good versus Evil! The whole reason we're here. The daemons and irins were put here to see who would recruit the most, and if Valefor steals a virtu from Luminelle, we have more."

"I thought they were tallying human souls. A virtu is not human," Wick contended, hoping to refute him somehow.

"Technically, she still is, until she takes the vows and accepts the gifts, but she's in such a unique position," Ava went on. "Luminelle can't make any more virtus. Once they're gone, they're gone forever." He snapped his fingers to emphasize his point. "It's always seemed like a horrible idea to me. Valefor can go on replacing us until the end of time. But that is approaching rather quickly."

"You think the whole world will end if Lily serves him?" Lux asked.

"The world as we know it, yes. That's what Valefor believes, anyway," Ava said. "And our Master is many things, but he is rarely wrong."

"She won't serve him," Wick said. "Lily would never serve a daemon."

"Maybe not," Ava agreed. "But she is in a perfect position. She doesn't even know *what* she is."

"What happens if she says no?" Lux asked.

Ava shrugged. "He'll kill her. Valefor has been feeling tired lately, and he's been trying to capture an irin for a good rejuvenation. But since she's a virtu, she'll do."

Valefor, like all daemons, was immortal, but over time, he'd weaken. Even at his lowest state, he'd still be more powerful than any of the peccati, but his skin would wrinkle, his hair would gray, and he'd have less energy. In order to maintain immortality, daemons and irins had to make sacrifices. Irins sacrificed many of the world's pleasures. Daemons sacrificed lives, stealing lifeforces to maintain their youth.

"In what scenario does he keep her alive?" Lux asked.

"He plans to wed her. He wants a bride to rule by his side, helping him take over all of Cormundie."

"What is Scelestus getting in return?" Wick asked.

Avaritia raised an eyebrow. "Pardon?"

"Queen Scelestus. She's the one that sold the Castimonia to your Master," Wick said. "What did she receive as payment?"

"Oh that. She wants to be the Invidia." Ava grinned. "She didn't even know what the girl was. She approached Valefor looking for a position, and after listening to her, he deduced that Scelestus was in possession of the Castimonia. He would've agreed to almost anything, but she had no idea what she was selling."

"Does Invidia know that he's about to be replaced?" Lux asked.

"I doubt it. But he's been so useless, he should've seen it coming." Ava clicked his tongue and shook his head. "He envies the most ridiculous things. He's always trying to steal my shoes! I know I have fantastic footwear, but he should be out coveting and garnering kingdoms, not apparel of another peccati."

"Where is Lily?" Lux asked.

"What?" Ava looked confused and dubious. "Why do you even care? What has gotten into you?

You're living in squalor, fighting Ira, and obsessing over some silly girl."

"I need you to tell me where she's at," Lux repeated.

"Why? So you can storm the castle and save the princess?" Ava waved his hands in the air, pretending to be impressed. "I hate to break it to you, Lux, but you're too weak and ridiculous to handle this on your own. Maybe if you grovel back to Valefor and help swing the Castimonia's heart his way, he'll let you live and enjoy the apocalypse."

"He won't have her," Lux said firmly.

Ava studied him, gauging his sincerity, then nodded. "I can see you're a serious man. I don't agree with your choices, but I admire your conviction." He looked from Lux to the wand in Wick's hand. "I can help you out if you can help me."

"You want the wand?" Wick asked incredulously. "You can't even use it. You don't have the magic for it."

"I don't want to *use* a wand." Avaritia scowled in disgust. "I have enough of my own magic, thank you. But that's the horn of a unicorn. It's a rarity."

"What would you give us for it?" Lux asked, and Wick shot him a look.

"It's not for sale," she snapped.

Ava grinned. "Come now. Everything has a price."

"You know what we want," Lux said, ignoring Wick.

"I can tell you where she's at," Ava said. "But I can't do anything more than that, no matter what you offer me."

"She's with Valefor, isn't she?" Wick asked.

"Perhaps." Ava shrugged. "Or perhaps he's hiding her somewhere safe."

"Tell us where she is," Lux demanded.

"*Tsk, tsk.*" Ava wagged his finger at him. "Horn first. Then I'll tell you what I know."

Lux sighed and held out his hand so Wick would give him her wand, but she held it to her chest.

"He doesn't know anything," Wick protested. "Or at least not any more than you do. Lily's with Valefor."

"No, you know a peccati took her." Ava's lips spread out in a smug smile. "But you don't know if she's made it to Valefor yet, or what Ira might be doing with her until then."

Wick and Lux exchanged a look. She didn't want to give up her wand, especially for tepid information at best. But Lux's eyes were afraid and imploring. They both needed to do what had to be done to get Lily.

Wick scoffed, and she handed her wand over to Lux.

"Thank you," Lux said quietly, but she turned away from him and muttered to herself about how ridiculous this all was.

She crossed her arms over her chest and watched from the corner of her eye as Lux took a step toward Ava. Ava rubbed his hands together, his eyes locked on the prize he'd won from them.

But he should've been paying more attention to Lux.

Lux moved swiftly, reaching out with his empty hand to grab Ava by the hair and jerk his head back. Before Ava could do more than gasp in surprise, Lux slammed him back against the wall. The unicorn horn was pressed against Ava's throat, the sharp tip ready to tear open his jugular.

"What is the Castimonia's name?" Lux demanded in an angry growl.

"*What*?" Bewildered, Ava looked beyond Lux's shoulder to Wick. She could only shrug because she had no idea what Lux was up to, either. "You know her name. Why are you asking me?"

"Because I want to make sure you never forget it," Lux said. "She's a person, with a name, and if you hurt her, I know every way to kill a peccati, and I'll be happy to do them all to you."

"Lily," Ava said. "Her name is Lily. But it's not me you need to worry about. She has to be at Valefor's lair by now."

"I told you that he didn't know anything," Wick said from behind them.

"And I still have your wand," Lux reminded her.

"I already told you everything I know," Ava complained, and Lux pushed hard on the wand, piercing his skin just slightly. "Kill me if you want, Lux, but it won't help you. It won't save her."

"We don't have time for this," Wick said, and Lux relented.

He stepped back from Ava, who immediately smoothed back his hair and began straightening out his clothes.

"Here." Lux handed the wand to Wick.

Ava left then, out the front door the same way he'd come on in. Wick gathered up a few more things they might use on their journey, and then she and Lux ventured out into the night, into the Necrosilvam.

CHAPTER TWENTY-FOUR

THE PECCATI CARRIED LILY over his shoulder. Her wrists and ankles were bound with rope, preventing her from fleeing or fighting him too hard. She screamed after he'd scorched Lux, and for the first hour or so, she'd kicked and bucked against him. Eventually, her body gave out in exhaustion, and she cried softly as he carried her.

It was from glimpses around Ira's thick arms, with her head hanging upside down, that she first saw Valefor's lair. Or at least she assumed that's what it was based on its foreboding appearance.

The lair was a twisting tower of black and crimson dragonstone. The jagged spire scraped the dark clouds above. Some of the walls were crumbling, as if damaged in long ago battles.

"Home sweet home," Ira said with a laugh as they reached the lair's moat. He moved Lily, resituating her on his shoulder, and she could hardly see anything but the ground below. Ira's feet travelled on dirty boards of the bridge crossing the murky water of the moat, and finally over the dragonestones of the tower floor.

The smell of brimstone was overwhelming. Ira had tied a gag in her mouth to silence her, and she coughed around it.

She heard Ira talking to the guards at the door, their voices booming and inhuman. The language they spoke sounded vaguely like what they spoke in Insontia, but she couldn't really understand it.

The little she could see of Valefor's lair did not look pleasant. The walls were covered in scratches and splashes of red that looked ominously like blood.

The hallway they traversed seemed to go on forever, then she heard a heavy door groan open, and she felt the heat blast her like an inferno. Fearing he meant to cook her, she fought harder against Ira, kicking at him with what little strength she had left.

Ira dropped her onto the ground with a painful thud, and she immediately scrambled to sit up. The room wasn't an oven, as she'd feared.

The walls were dark, stained with ash like the chimneys at her palace. A long fireplace ran along one wall, its fire blazing, but somehow, it gave off very little light, leaving the room dim. It was furnished with several chairs and a long table, all of them made out of black lava rock, so they glistened in the light of the flames.

"I'm going to take the gag from your mouth." Ira bent down in front of her, so they were eye to eye. "But if you scream, even once, I will knock out every one of your teeth. Do you understand me?"

Lily sat on the floor, her ankles bound underneath her, her wrists bound behind her back. Her dress was torn and ragged, and her skin was bruised and bloody. Dirt and sticks knotted her hair, and it hung in a mess around her face. She stared up at Ira, and since she had no choice, she grunted her compliance.

He ripped the cloth from her mouth with more force than necessary.

"Now, what do you say?" Ira asked as he grinned down at her.

Lily glared up at him. "You expect me to thank you? I will spit on your grave before I thank you, and then and only then will I thank you for doing the world a service by leaving it."

He laughed warmly, like they were old friends bantering. "Get it all out now. Because when my Master gets here, he won't allow that. He'll make you wish you had died back there with your boyfriend."

"If I ever get free, you will be the one that wished you had died." She forced herself to hold his gaze even though she wanted to crumble. But when she thought of what Lux endured for her, she found her strength.

Ira chuckled. "Valefor is going to eat you up." Still laughing, he walked toward the door.

"Where are you going?" she asked.

"As much as I'd love to see what the Master has in store for you, I have other business to attend to," Ira said as he opened the door. "But don't worry. He won't keep you waiting much longer."

The door closed loudly behind him, leaving Lily alone in the strange room in a daemon's lair. It was so hot, her skin was already slick with sweat, but that could work to her advantage. She wriggled her wrists, trying to slip out from the rope.

She'd just about gotten one hand free when the door on the other side of the room opened, and she lifted her head to see Valefor walking toward her.

CHAPTER TWENTY-FIVE

THE CREATURES IN THE NECROSILVAM usually didn't
mess with Wick anymore. They had learned that it
was pointless, but even she wasn't prepared for how
quiet the forest could be when she walked with Lux.
Around him, nothing made a sound.

It occurred to her that he was likely the most
powerful thing in the cursed wood right now. That
was only because of his Master, and she wondered
again if she was doing the right thing in teaming up
with him.

But she had to rescue Lily. She owed Cass that
much. And if that meant working with a servant of
Valefor, then so be it.

The sun was starting to rise over the Necrosilvam
as they reached the edge of it. The light allowed them
to get a better view of how far they'd really gone, and
how far they had left to go. Lux had started out
leading the way, but as they walked on, he'd begun to
lag.

At first, Wick thought it was because he was
purposely trying to sabotage the rescue mission and
slow them down. But soon she realized that he wasn't
as healed as he'd claimed to be.

"Why don't we take a break for a minute?" Wick
suggested.

Lux shook his head. "We have to keep moving."

"Not at the pace we're going." She stopped, and
he took another step before looking back. "Sit for a

minute. I have some ringa root that I can put on your leg. It will help you so we can go faster."

He paused, considering it before nodding reluctantly. Lux headed nearer to her and sat down on a large boulder. Kneeling before him, she rummaged through her bag, and she pulled out a gnarled, bright orange tuber – the root of a ringa plant. It had strong healing properties, which is why she'd brought it along.

"Roll up your pants," Wick said, and Lux did as he was told.

Lumps of bone were malformed under his skin, bulging out below the knee. His bones hadn't set themselves right where the other peccati had broken them.

Without warning him, Wick pulled out her knife and sliced open his leg above the bump. He howled and swore under his breath.

"You could've let me know you were doing that," Lux grimaced.

"Sorry," she said flatly. She snapped open the ringa root and held it over his fresh wound, letting the juice drip inside so it could do its work.

Ringa reduced pain quickly, and Lux relaxed a bit. She pulled a rag out of her bag and pressed it to his leg, holding the juice inside.

"It will take a few minutes for it to work fully," Wick said.

"Thank you," he said, and Wick looked up at him when she realized he'd meant it. She'd never known peccati to be grateful.

"How are you like this?" she asked, not hiding the confusion in her voice.

He leaned back and met her baffled gaze evenly. "Like what?"

"Kind. How can you be kind?"

"I …" He trailed off and shrugged. "I am as I've always been."

"How did you end up working for Valefor?"

"That was a very long time ago," Lux said, as if it answered the question.

"You *chose* to, though," Wick pressed on. "You chose to do this, to be the Luxuria."

He avoided her gaze when he answered, "Yes."

"Why?" she asked. "Why would anyone willingly choose to be in the service of something so evil?"

"It's not that simple."

He moved her hands off his leg and tried to stand up. His leg wasn't fully healed, but she wouldn't force him to sit down. Wick stayed crouched, watching him as he hobbled away, then she stood and followed him.

"I was engaged," Lux said when caught up with him.

"When you were still human, you mean?" she asked.

"Yes," he said. "I was the prince of a very large kingdom, the only son, and I was set to inherit it all. My father had arranged a marriage with the daughter of the neighboring land, so we could join them and become nearly unstoppable."

"What was your fiancée's name?" Wick asked.

He sighed. "The horrible truth of it is that I don't remember her name. I forgot about her long ago. But she had a younger sister, Saphron." He paused for a moment and licked his lips. "I fell in love with Saphron nearly the instant I met her. I tried to convince my father to let me marry her instead, but she was already betrothed to another."

145

Lux stepped carefully over the brambles of the Necrosilvam, and Wick noticed that his gait was almost back to normal. The ringa root worked rapidly on him.

"Saphron loved me in return," Lux went on. "Somehow, I think that made it worse. We began an affair, and we did our best to keep it secret, but eventually my betrothed found out. I'd expected her to call off the wedding, but she did something worse."

"Worse?"

"She had Saphron sent away and insisted we go ahead with our wedding," Lux said. "I was irate and heart broken, but my fiancée wanted to rule the most powerful kingdom, and she wouldn't let a thing like love stand in her way. In retribution, I decided to live a life of debauchery. I slept with everyone I could."

"You couldn't be with the one you loved, so you decided to sleep with everyone?" Wick asked dubiously.

"I was young, rich, and maybe a little spoiled," he said matter-of-factly. "I was also miserable, and I didn't know how else to act out. And truly, I only wished to avoid my nuptials. By the time she finally called the wedding off, the entire kingdom knew of my exploits."

Wick scoffed, and Lux stopped and turned back to face her.

"I'm not proud of what I did or who I was, but I won't make any apologies for it, either," he said.

"I never asked you to," Wick said evenly. "But you still haven't told me how you came to work for Valefor."

"After my arranged marriage fell through, my father banished me," he explained. "I'd ruined the greatest deal of his life, and he was pissed off. Not that I blame him. But I was left homeless and penniless. Saphron had married her intended, and I never saw her again.

"And then, Valefor found me." Lux turned and started walking again. "He'd heard of my conquests, and he offered me a job. I had no other prospects. No talent other than drinking, gambling, and seduction, and that was exactly the job he was offering. So I took it."

They'd reached the edge of the Necrosilvam, at the Weeping Waters. Lux stared out at the murky water, more quicksand than true liquid. It bubbled and oozed, and Wick knew the kinds of monsters that lived inside of it, ones that weren't threatened by mere peccati.

"But it's not a job," Wick argued. "Being a peccati is far more than an occupation. You *become* something else."

"Maybe you don't," Lux said finally, still staring out at the swamp. "Maybe Valefor only wants you to think you lose your heart and your humanity."

"I know you'd like to believe that," Wick said quietly, and he looked over at her. "But you sold your soul to a daemon. You *cannot* love."

Lux didn't respond. He turned toward the Weeping Waters, looking ready to kill any creature that crossed him.

CHAPTER TWENTY-SIX

THE MAN WHO ENTERED THE ROOM was unlike any Lily had ever seen. The first word that came to her mind was *perfect*.

He was shirtless under a black robe, revealing his rippled abs and strong chest. He was taller than Ira but not as hulking. There was a leanness to his power. His eyes were pale and framed by dark lashes, and his mouth was full and broad above a strong jaw. His lustrous hair landed on his midback, and it was a stunning shade of burnt honey.

He had certainly been chiseled by the gods, with a beauty so enchanting and sublime, Lily couldn't look away even though she wanted to. As he walked toward her, he smiled, and her breath caught in her throat.

"Do I frighten you?" Valefor asked in a voice that sounded like a lullaby.

"No."

Fear wasn't what she felt, but something equally primal. A desire so intense that it bordered on pain.

Lily had known attraction before, and the pull she felt for Lux had its own power. But this was unbridled lust, a ravenous want that consumed her, and left her breathless and entranced.

"Good." He crouched before her, and he even smelled enticing, like powdery iris and musky spice. "I'll untie you so we can talk like civilized folk."

His hands brushed up against her as he untied her, and his skin felt like flames. Her body trembled, and she had to fight the compulsion to lean into his touch.

"I thought you said you weren't afraid of me," he said, his voice low and right in her ear. She closed her eyes and let it rumble through her.

"Just because I'm not afraid of you doesn't mean I want you to touch me," Lily said, and she looked back over her shoulder at him. He lifted his head, so his burning eyes met hers, and she forced herself to lie: "You repulse me."

"I repulse you?" Valefor raised an eyebrow. Her hands were free, and she pulled them away quickly, rubbing the scrapes on her wrists.

"You killed the man I love," Lily said, and it was that reminder that quelled the raging desire inside her.

The thought of Lux, writhing and bleeding as Ira scorched him, was enough to steel her spine. Her body may have reacted to Valefor's unrivaled beauty, but her heart remained true. Broken, perhaps, because of what had befallen Lux, but it still belonged to him.

"Have I?" He stepped back from Lily, leaving her to untie the ropes around her ankles. "This must have been a very long time ago, since it's been quite a while since I have killed a man myself."

"You ordered his death, then." Lily pulled at the knots, trying to keep Valefor in her sights as he walked away from her.

"Perhaps," he admitted. He pulled out a chair and sat down in it, resting his arm on the table. "Who is this man I allegedly harmed?"

"Lux." She swallowed hard when she said his name, and Valefor laughed. "Why do you find humor in that?"

"Well, to begin with, Lux is my servant," he said. "And he is no man."

Lux had told her that he served a Master who made dark deals with her stepmother, and in his confrontation with Ira, she'd realized that they both served a daemon, and that neither of them were entirely human.

Valefor's admission wasn't surprising, and his eyes darkened with disappointment as he studied her. "You don't believe me?" he asked when she didn't respond.

"I believe you. It just doesn't matter."

"It doesn't matter?"

"No. I love him, and he loved me." She finally freed her ankles, and she stood. "And you took him from me."

"You are so naïve." Valefor tried for an expression that was likely meant to be sympathetic, but he only managed bored. "He doesn't love you. It was his job to fool you, to trick you into coming back with him. And he does it so well. I know. That's why I chose him."

"Maybe you did choose him," she said, trying to keep her voice even. "Maybe he was supposed to bring me to you. But he didn't. He cared for me more than he cared for serving you. That's why you sent Ira to stop him and take me away."

His face hardened, appearing even more like marble. It took all her will to keep from flinching and apologizing for defying a daemon such as him, but she thought of Lux and stood tall.

"You don't know who he is," Valefor said. "If you did, you wouldn't speak with such conviction."

"I love him, and nothing you can say will change that."

151

"Have you heard of the peccati?" he asked.

"They are minions in the service of daemons."

"Close, but it's not any daemon. Just me." He slowly stood, trailing his fingers along the table as he walked toward her. "There are seven peccati on Cormundie, each one meant to spread the good of a particular sin."

"The *good* of a sin?" Lily asked.

"In my line of work, sin is good," he purred as he smirked. "Lux happens to be my Luxuria. Do you know what that means?"

"No." She stared up at him, watching as he moved ever closer to her, but her feet felt cemented to the floor.

"Lust." His smile deepened. "Your love, your one and only, is my minion for lust. He was created to tempt the pure, to use his body to lead people astray." He stopped right in front of her, so close that the heat from his body warmed her skin, and she felt dizzy seeing his perfection so close.

"He never hurt me," Lily said, but the conviction in her voice was waning. "He *protected* me."

"That was his job. He left you untouched for me."

"He didn't leave me," she argued, and she stared up into the daemon's eyes. "And I am not untouched."

His lip curled in a snarl, but his voice was flat when he asked, "Pardon?"

"He did more than touch and tempt me," she said, steeling herself for the anger she saw burning in the daemon. "If what you need is some pure virgin, then I am of no use to you anymore."

"He's dead now, isn't he!" Valefor roared, and Lily shied away from his rage. His eyes blazed and the fire around the room grew bright and stronger, as if his hatred ignited it.

His voice returned to his earlier husky velvet, though his dismissive contempt remained. "Do you think a vessel becomes unworthy after a single use? Or even ten thousand? It does not matter if you fornicated with everyone in your entire kingdom. All that matters is that you are with me now."

"What do you want with me?" Lily asked, trying to hide the quaver in her voice. "Why did you bring me here?"

Valefor softened instantly. The flames around the room died down, and the anger in his eyes was replaced by some kind of twisted pleasure. He smiled again and leaned back against the table behind him.

"I had hoped we could get more acquainted first, and then I could ask you in a more romantic fashion," he said. "But there's no sense in being coy. I want to marry you."

CHAPTER TWENTY-SEVEN

THE SWAMP GURGLED AROUND THEM. Bubbles rose to the surface, and when they popped, the noise that came out sounded like a child crying. Hence the name of Weeping Waters, and the bog had led many unsuspecting travelers to their deaths.

Lux and Wick made their way carefully across the swamp, using stones, trees, and the occasional patch of land to avoid stepping in the sludge. Touching the water wouldn't mean certain death in itself, but both of them knew the source of the weeping bubbles.

Hidden beneath the murky film were fish the size of grown men with teeth like blades, waiting to snap at anything that entered the water. They made the crying sound, sending it out in to lure someone to rescue a child that did not exist. Like a siren song, they called to their prey, tricking them into becoming a meal.

Wick led the way because she told Lux she'd traversed it many times, which he thought was absolute insanity. Once across the wretched water was more than enough. It reeked of putrid decay and death, and the crying call of the fish was maddening.

A massive tree had tipped over in the center of the swamp, and its large roots were splayed out above the surface, thick as tree trunks themselves. When they reached it, Wick stopped, standing on a large rock that jutted out of the swamp, and Lux stood on the rock behind her.

"What's wrong?" he asked, keeping his voice low. The creatures in the water listened for any sound, any reason to leap from the water.

"It didn't used to be like this." She motioned to the overturned tree in front of them. "Below the tree used to be a small island. It was a respite in the middle of the swamp, where you could catch your breath without fear of being eaten alive."

"Where's the island now?" Lux asked.

Wick shook her head. "When the tree went over, the island must've gone with it."

"We still have to go across. Island or not."

Instead of replying to that, Wick bent down and slid off her shoes. They were little more than cloth, more like socks or slippers than true shoes, and they had nothing to grip with on their bottoms. She put the shoes in her satchel, then reached out carefully and stepped onto the root in front of her.

Since they were roots, they were smoother and slicker than the fallen logs they had used as steppingstones. Some of them were even covered in mud or moss, making them even more slippery. While most of the roots were quite thick, not all of them were. Climbing over them meant utilizing narrow roots, ones that might even snap under their weight.

There was no other way through the swamp, unless they backtracked and went around the Weeping Waters, and they didn't have time for that.

Lux followed suit and slipped off his own shoes. His were newer and far nicer than Wick's, but they didn't have soles for gripping. He didn't have a satchel to put them in, so he tucked them into the back of his pants and went after her.

Wick moved nimbly from one root to the next, and Lux was surprised by her agility. He had to struggle to keep up with her.

Until she'd made it near the top. She jumped from one root to the next, and though she landed it, her foot slipped on a patch of moss, and she fell.

"Wick!" Lux yelled, and she caught herself before she tumbled into the water.

With one arm wrapped around the root, she dangled above the swamp, and her bare feet were mere inches from the surface.

"I'm okay," she said breathlessly. She tried to pull herself up, but her arm slipped and she almost fell again.

He scrambled across the roots, hurrying to get to her. "I'll pull you up. Just hang on."

"Be careful," she warned him. "You can't help me if you fall in."

Lux followed her advice but he had to move fast. Her grip on the branch seemed tenuous, and he could see her satchel slipping from her shoulder. If that fell into the water, the fish would leap out after it and bite onto Wick, maybe even pulling her into the murky depths.

She wrapped one arm tightly around the root, securing herself as best she could, and let go with her other arm. But when she did, her balance shifted. Her bag tilted, and one of her shoes slipped out and tumbled toward the swamp.

"No," Wick whispered, as the shoe splashed into the muck.

Lux reached her and grabbed her hand just as he saw a monstrous fish cresting the water.

It was the size of a bison, and it leapt out of the swamp. Long tentacles protruded out of each of its

sides, like overgrown catfish whiskers, quickly
propelling it through the muddy swamp. When the
fish opened its mouth, it was like a giant bear trap that
barely missed Wick's feet.

Lux pulled her onto the root next to him, and they
both knelt there for a minute, catching their breath.
Before the first fish had even landed back in the
water, another one had jumped out. Within seconds,
there was a frenzy of them, jumping and biting at the
air just below where Lux and Wick were.

"Thank you," Wick panted, but she didn't look at
Lux when she said it.

"Not letting a monster fish eat you seemed like
the least I can do."

The crying of the fish had gotten even louder,
like a choir of screaming children. One of the fish
leapt out even farther, snapping off the end of the root
they rested on.

"I think we should go," he said.

As they climbed onward, most of the fish stayed
behind, hunting in the spot where the shoe had fallen,
but a few followed. Lux could see the bubbles trailing
them as they moved.

CHAPTER TWENTY-EIGHT

"YOU WANT TO MARRY ME?" Lily asked the daemon incredulously. "Why would you ever want to marry someone like me? Because I would rather die than wed you!"

"Ordinarily, I would offer to arrange that for you, but not this time." Valefor waved his hand, completely unfazed by her reaction. "You will marry me. Maybe not today, and I understand that. You are confused and mourning the Luxuria who fooled you."

"I am not confused, and you killed him!" Lily shot back.

"No, I did not. I merely sent Ira to retrieve you, by any means necessary," he explained reasonably. "Lux killed himself by not getting out of my way. I needed to get you here with me. I had to know you were safe. I only did that to protect you."

She shook her head. "To protect me? From what?"

"From Lux!" He gestured to her. "He had you under a spell, and I only relied on him because it was so imperative that I got you away from your stepmother. She came to me because she wanted you dead, but I saw the beauty in you."

She narrowed her eyes at him. "How? How could you have seen me? We've never met before, and I would've known if someone like you came to the palace."

"Queen Scelestus showed me in her cauldron." He walked as he spoke, making a languid circle around her, and she stayed in place, staring straight ahead. "She told me of her husband's mousy child. Someone so boring and bland she could hardly even be considered a nuisance.

"And yet, somehow, such an unworthy slug managed to raise so much ire in the woman who was supposed to love you." He paused and leaned toward her, whispering in her ear as if sharing a secret. "And how Queen Scelestus loathed you. She even requested that I torture you before I kill you."

Nothing he said was surprising, but the truth in his words stung all the same. Lily did her best to mask her pain when she said, "Her dislike of me was hardly a secret. This is no revelation but being around you is certainly a torture all its own."

He smirked, then started walking again. "But this had my interest piqued," he continued, as if she hadn't spoken. "How could one child be both nothing and everything wrong in the world?

"And so, I asked her to show you to me." He stopped right in front of her, and he put a hand to his chest. "As soon as I saw you, I knew."

"Knew what?" Lily asked, despite herself.

"That you were meant to be my bride," he said, sounding almost wistful.

She shook her head in dismay. "Why? Why me? Undoubtedly there are girls lovelier and wealthier and more wicked than I. And you are a powerful handsome daemon. You can have anyone in all of Cormundie. What could I possibly have to offer someone like you?"

"I am happy to see you understand the situation perfectly," he said with a satisfied exhalation. "I can have anyone I want, and I have chosen you."

"*Why?*" she repeated, disbelieving.

"Why would I not?" He stepped closer to her. Lily held her breath as he gently caressed her face, and heat flushed over her. "Are you not lovely enough? Kind enough? Do you not have your own charms to share? Your own love to give?"

"Yes," she admitted softly, and for a moment, his eyes were all she could see. But she blinked and thought of Lux. "But I could never love you."

He frowned and dropped his hand. "I know this is a bad time. I will let you get settled in, and we can talk more later, when you've had more time to clear your head."

"I will never marry you. You're the devil!"

Valefor smiled. "No, I'm not, but thank you. I do appreciate the comparison. Lily, my darling, I understand your anger here," he said. "Really, I do. But you haven't heard what I have to offer you. You could be anything you wanted. I would give you everything your heart desires."

She met his gaze and told him honestly, "Lux is the only thing my heart desires. Will you return him to me?"

Valefor merely smiled sadly down at her. She'd thought his rage might flare up again, but he only nodded.

"If there's one thing I've learned living on Cormundie for the past millennia, it's that young hearts are transient things," he said. "You will forget him. And then you will truly understand what I am giving you.

"But I'm tired of this conversation now." He turned and headed toward the door. "It's time you see your quarters."

Lily didn't think – she just charged at him. All the calm she'd been fighting to hold onto disappeared into an angry, desperate attempt to save herself and avenge Lux. Throwing the rope from her ankles around his neck, she jumped onto his back, trying to choke him.

He didn't even struggle. He grabbed the rope and tore it in half with hardly an effort. He elbowed her in the stomach, knocking her to the ground. She cradled her belly, gasping for breath, and she barely stopped herself from vomiting.

"I am sorry for that, darling, but you made me do it." Valefor looked down at her. "You do understand that, don't you?"

She coughed because she couldn't speak, and he sighed. As she lay on the ground in pain, he opened the door and summoned his guards to take her away. Two large ogres came in to get her, towering over Valefor. They grabbed Lily by the arms because she couldn't stand yet, and they dragged her out of the room.

CHAPTER TWENTY-NINE

"THESE DAMN FISH ARE DRIVING ME MAD," Lux muttered.

"Just ignore them," Wick said, but that was easier said than done. The constant shrieking broke through his every thought, and it made his head throb.

"I'm trying to," he said, and no sooner had the words left his mouth than the fish calls quieted down. They were still crying, but more subdued.

"It's already getting better," she said, climbing onto the root in front of her. "And we're almost to the other side of the tree." She pointed in front of her to where a bit of the island still remained. "It's not that much farther until we're out of the swamp."

"I will feel so much better on stable land," he said.

"There should be another smaller island on the other side of that one," she explained as they made their way toward it. "And then a few logs, some rocks, and we're out."

Lux stopped and tilted his head, listening to the growing silence. "Wick."

"Things might have changed, but that's the way I remember them anyway," she went on.

"*Wick*," he repeated, louder this time.

"What?" She turned around to face him, annoyed, but realization slowly dawned on her, and Lux knew she heard it too.

Nothing. The crying had stopped completely. The only reason the fish would be quiet was if a creature more dangerous was around.

In the silence, it was easy to hear the slurping of something big moving through the swamp. Lux looked behind them just in time to see the hump of a creature above the water, its back covered in dark green scales with razor-sharp fins along the spine, and then it disappeared into the water again.

"Run," Wick commanded, but he was already going.

They moved as fast as they could and leapt from the tree onto the island. It was wet and muddy, and both of them fell when they landed. Lux had barely gotten up when the sea dragon lurched out of the water. It crashed right into the island, sending a muddy water wave rolling over them.

The sea dragon's head was large enough that it could swallow Lux whole if it wanted to, with a neck longer than he was tall. Below that were clawed feet on two very short arms. Its body was long and thin, more serpentine than the land dragons. The swamp water couldn't stick to its skin, so the iridescent green scales that covered the beast shimmered brightly.

"I hate dragons," Lux complained as he scrambled to his feet.

In response, the creature fixed its golden eyes on them, then opened its mouth and let out a loud roar. Along with that, fire blasted out from the dragon's mouth.

Lux moved in between Wick and the dragon, shielding her as best he could. The flames singed the back of his neck, but the shirt she'd given him was impervious to dragonfire, like his skin. He ran faster, pushing her along.

Wick ran across rocks like steppingstones, with Lux and the dragon right on her tail. He didn't turn back, but he could hear the beast crashing through everything behind them. It was quick in the water but lumbered on land, so their only chance at escaping it was to make it to dry land.

A weeping willow was in front of them, and Wick grabbed onto one of its long branches, using it to swing across. Lux reached for one and slipped, so he settled for grabbing onto a branch and climbing up the tree, toward the trunk where its branches were stronger.

The dragon dove under the water, disappearing for a moment, and Lux could see Wick, standing on a giant boulder.

"Do you have anything to stop a sea dragon?" Lux shouted down at Wick.

"The only way to stop a dragon is to stab it through its heart," the witch said. "Get out of the tree before it comes back!"

Lux stood on one of the weaker branches and slid down it toward Wick and the boulder. Just when he got close, the sea dragon sprung out of the water, opening its jaws in front of him so Lux was posed to slide right into its mouth.

Thinking fast, Lux used the branch like a springboard and jumped up over the creature's head. When he landed on the rock with a painful thud, the dragon let out an angry roar.

Wick pulled him to his feet, and they were running again. The dragon crashed down in the water next to them, making the rocks they had to cross slick and wet. Lux could feel the heat from the fire behind him when the dragon rose out of the water.

They were close enough where they could actually see the shore. There was a gap between the rocks and land, too far for them to jump. But an old tree grew out of the dry land, hanging over the swamp. Wick leapt forward and grabbed onto a low-hanging branch, and then swung herself across to the shore.

Lux meant to do the same, but when he grabbed the branch, it broke, and he and the branch fell into the water. The good news, if there was any, was that the water wasn't as deep here. It only came up past his waist, and with the dragon here, all the fish were too afraid to attack.

The dragon arched itself out of the water, staring down at Lux, and he had nowhere to go. The muddy water was too thick for him to outrun it and the dragon seemed to know that. Its yellow eyes glinted with victory, and Lux clenched the broken branch in his hand.

When the dragon roared again in his face, Lux didn't back down. He was so close that the beast's breath blew back his hair. He could hear Wick shouting behind him, telling him to run or fight or do *something*. But he didn't move. Not until the dragon opened his mouth to breathe fire on him.

Lux crouched down, so the branch was safely below the water, and he let the flames go over his flesh. He didn't burn, and the dragon lost sight of him in its breath. Once the fire covered him, Lux ducked down, submerging himself below the water, and using all his might, he churned through the thick swamp.

He came up right in front of the dragon's chest. Lux rammed the branch right into its heart. It roared and thrashed around, letting out a few last puffs of smoke before collapsing. Its body splashed in the water but the head crashed onto the shore, a few feet from where Wick stood.

It would only be a matter of moments before the fish caught on that the dragon had become a free meal, so Lux hurried toward the land as fast as he could. Wick was waiting for him, and she held out her hand and helped him onto the shore.

"I really hate dragons," he reiterated once he was safely out of the swamp.

"But you're invulnerable to dragonfire," Wick said, handing him a cloth so he could wipe the putrid water from his face.

"Just because I can't be burned doesn't mean that I enjoy it." He cleaned himself off, then gave her the cloth back. "Thank you."

He turned to start walking away, to continue on their trek, when Gula stepped out from a patch of trees. He glowered down at Lux and crossed his arms firmly over his chest.

"And just where do you think you're going?" Gula demanded.

CHAPTER THIRTY

LILY HAD FALLEN UNCONSCIOUS on her way down to her new quarters, and she woke up in the worst pain of her life. Her eyes were swollen from crying in her sleep, and they opened slowly. In the dim light, she saw a birdcage hanging above her.

Somehow she was home, in her parents' chambers in the Insontian palace, where her mother's canary sang a cheerful song as she flew about the room.

But Lily blinked, and the chambers vanished. Instead it was a dank cave that reeked of death.

"Easy now, you don't want to hurt yourself," a small voice said as Lily tried to sit up. She glanced around, but she didn't see whoever had just spoken to her.

Her room was carved into stone, but the bars across the front made it a cell. Skeletons littered the dirty floor around her, and she scrambled away from them. But there was nowhere to go, and her back slammed into a cold, rough wall.

Her sudden movements startled the only living occupant that she could see – a black unicorn stallion. He was a huge beast, much larger than her horses back in Insontia. An iridescent obsidian horn grew from between his two big eyes.

Despite his size, he seemed terrified of her – letting out an anxious neigh as he stomped his feet.

"Be calm, Addonexus," a satin voice said from another cell. But it still wasn't the tiny voice she'd heard when she first awoke here.

In the cell across the corridor, an irin was locked up. He was a handsome man with dark brown skin and bright white feathered wings. He was shirtless, with a wing torn badly where it connected to his back, his muscles exposed and his feathers stained red with blood. Despite that, he reached his arm through the bars to comfort the unicorn.

Lily had never been near an irin before, and he was utterly beautiful, as she'd always heard them described. Even in the dim light, he seemed to glow. There was something luminous about him.

"What happened to you?" Lily asked.

"The same thing that always happens around here." That was the small voice again. "Up here. In the cage."

A thin, greenish arm reached between the bars of the birdcage and waved at her. Lily stood up so she could get a better look, and she saw a little woodsprite, no more than two feet tall. Their green hair stuck up all over, with vines and leaves growing out from it.

"What always happens?" Lily asked.

"*Valefor.*" The sprite sighed and rested their forehead against the bars of the cage. "He tortures and kills until he gets what he wants."

"What does he want from you?"

"He wants me to tell him where my village is so he can capture us all and turn us into stew." The sprite's brown eyes were wide and earnest. "But I won't tell him. No matter what he does to me."

"Are you okay?" Lily asked the sprite.

"I'm as well as any woodsprite locked in a tiny cage would be," they said.

Lily sat on the floor and ripped off some fabric of her dress near the hem. Then she extended her arm between the bars and out into the narrow corridor that separated her from the irin, offering it to him. "For your wounds."

"Thank you." He smiled as he took it, and he pressed the cloth against the wounds on his back and wing.

"What does Valefor want with you?" she asked him.

"To drink my blood. It makes him more powerful. And *that* –" he pointed to the unicorn pacing the far side of her cell, "– that is what he means to kill me with."

Lily was aghast. "A unicorn?"

"The horn of a living unicorn piercing the heart is the best way to kill an irin," he explained. "Valefor's had me trapped down here for days, holding me captive until he could find a suitable weapon. His servants brought that one in this morning."

As if knowing they were talking about him, the horned beast brayed and reared on its back legs. It came down heavily, crushing a skull beneath its hooves.

"You are safe for now, Addonexus." The irin held up his hand, and Lily noticed something in his voice. It had taken on a more silken quality, soothing her. She'd heard that irins had that power, that they calm mortals with words and elate them with their songs, but she'd never spoken to one before.

"The unicorn's name is Addonexus?" Lily asked once the horse had calmed.

"That's what we've been calling him," the irin said. "It means 'bringer of death.'" Her eyes widened, and he laughed softly. "It's a bit of gallows humor."

"Quite literally," she murmured.

"I am Tarragon," the woodsprite said, then pointed to the irin. "He is Aeterna."

"Lily." She gave them both a small smile. "I'm sure it'd be a pleasure to meet you both if it weren't under such dire circumstances."

"Yes, I'm certain it would be," Aeterna agreed, returning her smile.

"How come you haven't asked me what Valefor wants with me?" Lily asked.

"Because I already know. He means to marry you." His eyes were so dark, nearly black, and they were solemn when he looked upon her.

"Is he that obvious?" Lily asked in surprise, then realized that the irin might know more about her situation than she did. "Why does he want marriage with me?"

"You are the Castimonia," Aeterna said.

"What?" Lily shook her head. "I'm not … I'm only the Princess of Insontia…" She started to deny it, but something stirred inside her.

As he said the word "Castimonia," she'd known it was her name. There was a wave of understanding flooding through her, illuminating all the dark crevices of her life.

Suddenly, a memory returned, from when she was very young and her mother was still alive. Her mother had been holding her, singing to her, and she smiled radiantly down at her.

"You may yet be so small, but your heart is so big. You have so much love and power inside you, my sweet Castimonia."

"But how…" Lily stared through the bars at Aeterna. "How could you know? I've taken no vows, and I didn't even know what I am. How?"

"Because I am an irin," he said with a modest smile. "It's something that I can sense."

"How can she be the Castimonia if she does not know?" Tarragon asked, voicing Lily's own confusion.

"Peccati are a choice humans make, but virtus are born," Aeterna explained. "She has always been the Castimonia, even before she knew anything at all. It is who she is."

"What does Valefor want with a virtu who doesn't yet know her powers?" Tarragon asked.

"He wants Lily to take her vows to him," Aeterna reasoned. "If he does that, he wins. He'll have turned a virtu to his side. Evil will triumph over Good."

"But I will never serve him," she argued. "Can't I take my vows to Luminelle? Then won't this all be over?"

"Yes… if Luminelle were here," Aeterna said. "You have to give them to her, when you're in her presence."

"You're an irin. Can't I give my vows to you?" she asked.

"No. I am merely a messenger. I do the bidding of my Masters, like Luminelle, and I help the mortal animals."

"You were working when Valefor caught you?" she asked.

He nodded. "I was meant to help the other virtus find you. We had gotten word that Valefor had plans to turn the missing Castimonia, and everything on Cormundie seems to sense that something is amiss. The canu snuck up on me in a way they never have before. My wings were broken in the struggle, and they captured me."

"I'm so sorry for all you've been through," Lily said.

"She's just a child," Tarragon said, their voice even smaller with despair. "She doesn't stand a chance against the torture the daemon will inflict on her."

"Tarragon, come now," Aeterna chastised the sprite. "She's the Castimonia, the strongest of heart. If anyone stands a chance against Valefor, it's her."

"How can you be so certain?" she asked. "I am caged, and everyone who tries to help me has been hurt. What am I to do in the face of the most powerful daemon in all the kingdoms of Cormundie?"

"Lily." Aeterna used his soothing tone, calming her. "You can't let fear or guilt eat away at you. You are good, and you need to remember that above all else. Love is stronger than hatred, and you are made of love."

She took a deep, fortifying breath, and then lifted her head, meeting his gaze evenly. "I won't let him take over the world.

CHAPTER THIRTY-ONE

"GET BACK!" WICK YELLED and dug in her satchel, pulling out her wand before the behemoth of a peccati could assault them.

She'd never seen him before, but she smelled the sulfur on him. He was tall and thick, with hands bigger than her own head. His eyes were a brilliant green, and they seemed to be smirking down at her.

Wick moved in front of Lux, preparing to defend him. She'd seen what Ira had done to him, and after Lux had saved her life — *twice* — she felt she owed him the same courtesy.

"Whoa, easy!" The thick peccati held up his massive hands and took a step back. His frown turned to fear and surprise. "I was only joking!"

"Wick, it's okay." Lux put his hand on her arm, pressing it gently so she would lower her wand, and she glanced between the two of them. "Gula is a friend of mine."

"But the peccati are sent to get you, by any means necessary," Wick reminded him harshly. She lowered her wand, but her grip on it tightened, in case she needed to use it.

Lux looked back at his alleged friend. "What are you doing here?"

"Valefor wants you dead, and he wants to marry your girlfriend, though I'm not sure he cares about the order they happen. I thought you could use some help," Gula said amiably.

175

"You don't need to go up against Valefor. His sights are set only on me," Lux said.

"I know. But I always liked you more than him," Gula said with a shrug.

Lux laughed at that, and he went over to pat Gula on the back. "It's good to have you on my side."

"Wait," Wick said in dismay. "What?"

"What?" Lux looked back at her.

"You're just taking his word on that?" she asked dubiously and gestured to the larger peccati. "He could be a spy for Valefor! He could intend to sabotage us!"

"You don't know Gula," Lux said simply.

"I'm Gula." He stuck out his hand, meaning to introduce himself to Wick, and she crossed her arms, refusing to take it. "I'm gluttony. I like to eat and drink and enjoy myself. I don't like hurting anyone."

She shook her head. "It's bad enough that I have to put trust into Lux. I'm not taking on another peccati. That's just dancing with the devil."

"Wick." Lux sighed. "I don't have time to argue with you. But you don't know what we're up against. Having someone with Gula's strength and stature might be the only way we get into Valefor's lair. If you want to rescue Lily, this is our best chance."

Wick didn't want to follow him, but she also knew she didn't really have a choice. He knew Valefor's lair better than she did, and if he was right about needing Gula's strength, then there would be no way she could do it on her own.

Reluctantly, she walked with them, but she kept a few steps behind. Just in case.

"How did you know where I'd be?" Lux asked Gula.

"Ava told me he found you in the Necrosilvam," Gula said. "The quickest way from the Necrosilvam to Valefor is through the Weeping Waters. I couldn't manage that swamp myself, so I thought I'd wait for you on the other side. Nice job with that dragon, by the way."

"You saw me fighting a dragon but didn't step in?" Lux raised an eyebrow.

Gula shrugged. "You had it under control. And I hate dragons."

"So do I," Lux muttered. "Where did you see Ava?"

"He tracked me down at the bar to gloat about how awful you were doing. He said that Ira had beaten you to a pulp and you were working with a hag." He glanced back at Wick. "Sorry. Those were his words, not mine. I personally think you're much too lovely to be a hag."

Wick snorted at his compliment, and Lux laughed.

They walked on, but things were much easier past the Weeping Waters. Gula and Lux talked some, and Wick listened but didn't add anything. She kept her pace a few steps behind them and couldn't wait for all this to be over. Working with peccati made her edgy.

They reached a clearing with a babbling brook running through it. Jagged rocks stood on the other side, and above that, the red tower where Valefor lived. The air smelled thickly of brimstone, and Wick held a cloth in front of her face.

"That reminds me," Gula said when he saw Wick blocking the smell. "You need to get cleaned up."

"Why?" Lux asked. "We're almost there."

"But you were submerged in the swamp, and you smell like it," Gula said. "If you expect us to get past the ogres at the door, we'll need the element of surprise, and you reek like fish and sea dragons."

"Fair enough."

Gula sat on a rock near the brook, and Lux waded into the water, where it was deep enough for him to wash up. When he pulled off his shirt, Wick only looked at him long enough to see the burn mark in his chest was almost fully healed. Then she lowered her gaze so she wouldn't be staring at his taut physique.

"Lux was never really that bad," Gula said, his voice quiet so Lux couldn't hear.

Wick glanced over at the giant man sitting beside her. "What?"

"He was never cut out for this," Gula elaborated. "Not really. He liked nice things and parties, but that's about as evil as he gets. And he's loyal. He's stood up for me to Valefor many times."

"He stood up to Valefor?" Wick asked skeptically.

"Well, nobody stands up to Valefor," Gula qualified. "But when our Master would think of doing away with me, Lux would point out all the things I had done, and he would ask Valefor to assign me on missions with him, so I'd have something that made me look useful."

"Why?" Wick asked and turned to face him. "Why would Lux do that? Why would he do anything for anyone that wasn't himself?"

"We joined Valefor about the same time, and we've always had each other's back. We've seen other peccati come and go, but we've both remained."

"How long have you worked for Valefor?"

"Oh, I don't know." Gula thought and shook his head. "Decades."

"Decades?" She gaped at him.

Both peccati and virtus were immortal when in the service of their Masters. They would not age past young adulthood, never growing old. The only way they finished their duty was if they were killed or bowed out, but bowing out was not an option for Valefor. Nobody left him.

Wick knew that, and she'd even known that Cass was over a century old when she retired from her role as the Castimonia to marry Lily's father and start a family. But from the way Lux had so quickly turned on his Master, she hadn't thought him more than a few years as the Luxuria.

Lux had finished washing and stepped out of the stream. He shook his head, shaking out the cold droplets of water from his hair.

"What do you say we go rescue Lily?" he asked.

The water seemed to refresh him, and he trekked up the jagged rocks. Wick followed close behind him, though she couldn't match his pace.

There was an easier way to the lair: a road that led right to the front door. But if they took that path, Valefor would see them coming a mile away.

Lux led the way through a secret passage under the moat. "Valefor had this made for the canu, so they can sneak out and catch unsuspecting prey," he said, but she hadn't really needed the explanation. The tunnel smelled of canu dung, and there were bones all over with meat hanging off.

Wick noticed with some disgust that there was a chewed-up irin wing on the ground. Most of the meat was missing, but the feathers remained.

The passage branched off in several directions, so the canu had many different places to exit. The one that Lux chose opened up right below the bridge in front of the main gate.

"Valefor has used this many times to get a jump on anyone trying to invade his lair," Lux said as he peered up at the bridge. "Now all I have to do is climb up on the bridge and get rid of the two massive ogres blocking our entry to the tower."

CHAPTER THIRTY-TWO

ADDONEXUS REARED ON HIS BACK LEGS, and even Aeterna's soothing voice had no effect on him. The irin straightened himself up and tried to stand, but the lame wing made him off balance, and he leaned against the bars.

By then, Lily heard what had spooked the unicorn. The clicking of hooves on the dungeon floor, and a horrible hissing breath. She didn't know what they were, but she could see the terror in the unicorn's eyes.

"Be strong," Aeterna said.

"Don't let them know that you're afraid," Tarragon added in a trembling voice.

As the footfalls grew closer, Lily peered through the bar with wide eyes, and she asked softly, "What are they?"

"Sonneillons," Aeterna answered. "They are daemons of hate, lesser minions of Valefor. They thrive on torture."

Lily swallowed hard and held her head high. Even when the sonneillons appeared in front of the cell door, and she bit her tongue to keep from crying out in horror, she refused to show any fear.

They were hideous creatures unlike any she'd ever seen before. They walked hunched over, and yet they were still taller than either Lily or Aeterna. Their skin was burgundy leather, and it appeared to be peeling in many places, revealing putrid green patches

181

underneath. Small horns jutted out from their skulls near the front. Short, black hair covered their scalps and grew down the backs of their necks until it stopped between their shoulders.

They were thin to the point of emaciation. The bumps of their spine looked like spikes down their backs. Small, bright yellow eyes seemed to glow from their sunken faces, and rows of razor- sharp teeth filled their mouths. Though they had the legs of a man, they had the cloven hooves of a beast.

But the thing that Lily found the most horrifying was their hands. Their fingers were unnaturally long, growing nearly a foot. At the tips were black fingernails like hooked talons. One of the sonneillons reached between the bars, extending his lengthy arm so he nearly touched Lily.

Both of them wore little in the way of clothing, a ragged vest on one, something like pants on the other. But they both had a belt around the waists, with a keyring and golden rope hanging from it.

"She smells delicious," the first sonneillon said. His voice had a strange vibrato to it, and a vileness that sent chills down Lily's spine.

"I want to dine on her flesh," he added, and a narrow-forked tongue flitted out of his mouth.

"We're not here for her, Cifer," the other one snapped, and the first sonneillon pulled back his hand. "We can have scraps of the irin when we're done."

"Yes, I suppose that will do, Beeze," Cifer said, and his hungry gaze went from Lily to the frightened unicorn.

Beeze used a large key carved from an irin's bone that he twisted in the lock to open it. Lily recognized it as irin bone because it was pure white and sparkled like diamonds.

"You will dine on nothing," Lily said, her voice as strong as she could make it. "You will starve to death before I let you eat anything in this room."

Both of the sonneillons laughed, a horrible cackling sound that echoed off the walls of the dungeon. Tarragon crouched down and covered their ears, while the unicorn brayed and stomped the ground.

"Lily," Aeterna said quietly, "they are not here for you. Don't anger them."

"Listen to your friend," Beeze suggested and opened her cell. "He knows too well what we can do."

"No." Lily stepped forward, moving in front of Addonexus. "You will not take him."

"Cifer." Beeze narrowed his eyes at Lily, so they were merely slits of yellow light. "Move her."

"With pleasure." The sonneillon smiled widely, revealing all the teeth in his horrible mouth.

With surprising speed, he charged on Lily. He growled and back handed her, his claws tearing across her face. She flew back on the floor, crashing into the skeletons near Addonexus. The unicorn reared, and Lily barely moved in time to avoid being crushed under the animal's hooves.

"Get the beast before he kills her!" Beeze commanded. "The Master will not be pleased if she is destroyed."

Beeze tossed a rope to Cifer, who walked cautiously toward the unicorn. He held up his hands in a gesture of peace, but Addonexus was not fooled. He slammed his massive frame into the wall, his shoulder driving into stone. But the unicorn couldn't get away. He could only stomp his feet and neigh in anger.

"Leave him alone!" Lily shouted and rushed to her feet. She ran at Cifer, jumping at his back, even though it revolted her to touch his peeling flesh. He knocked her off with ease and kicked her back with one of his cloven feet.

Lily lay on the ground, surrounded by the remains of others who had not escaped. She looked over at Aeterna. Beeze had turned the golden rope into a noose, and Aeterna wore it around his neck.

"Move!" Beeze yanked on the rope so the irin would rise. The sonneillon meant to take him away like that, walking him on the noose like a dog on a leash.

A great and glorious irin would be dragged around by a cackling sonneillon. The very thought of it broke Lily's heart.

As Aeterna struggled to his feet, hampered by the rope around his neck and his broken wing, Cifer continued fighting with the unicorn. Addonexus would not calm, and Cifer wouldn't move closer until he did.

"Everything will be all right, Lily." Aeterna tried to comfort Lily as Beeze pulled him into the dungeon corridor. "Just remember what I told you."

Tears stung her eyes, and she turned back to Addonexus and Cifer. The animal was crying, and Lily had no idea how to help him.

"Cifer!" Beeze yelled. "Hurry up and get the beast! The Master is waiting!"

"I am trying!" Cifer snapped. He stepped toward Addonexus, but when the unicorn reared up, Cifer stepped back again.

That's when Lily realized the sonneillon was afraid of the horned horse. She sat up, her eyes locked on the unicorn's.

"Addonexus," Lily said, keeping her voice as calm and even as she could. She wasn't even sure unicorns could understand her, or if Addonexus would listen to her if he did. But she had to try. "Addonexus, listen to me. He has no power over you. You are stronger than him. You can stop him."

"Shut up, you wench!" Cifer yelled and kicked a broken skull at her.

But Addonexus's black eyes stayed on hers, and he stopped moving. He stood still and snorted once, but that was all.

"Get the horse, you fool!" Beeze told Cifer. "It is calmed!"

Cifer moved toward the unicorn. Just as he did, Addonexus suddenly turned to look at him. Before the sonneillon could do anything more, the unicorn charged at him and ran him straight through with his horn. Cifer made an anguished sound, and his body spasmed once before he fell still.

"Vile wench!" Beeze shouted as Cifer's bloody corpse slid off the unicorn's horn and onto the ground.

Addonexus turned his attention to Beeze, who slammed the door shut before the unicorn could get him.

Aeterna saw that they might have a chance to escape, so he unfurled his good wing and batted Beeze with it. It didn't hurt him really, but it knocked him off guard for a moment. That was all the time he needed.

He grabbed the key made of irin bone, hanging off the sonneillon's belt. Beeze hissed in anger, and Aeterna raised the key high and then slammed it down into the sonneillon's eye.

They both fell to the ground, the sonneillon landing on top of the irin. The blood from the daemon's eye socket spilled out into him, and Aeterna pushed him off and got up.

Tarragon's cage hung from the ceiling by a rope attached to the wall. The irin key was cut with jagged ridges, making it almost like a serrated knife. Lily took the key from Aeterna, and then went over to the rope and started sawing through it.

Aeterna stood by the open cell door, keeping lookout. Lily finally got through the rope enough, and Tarragon's cage clattered to the floor.

"Tarragon!" Lily exclaimed and knelt down next to the cage. "Are you all right?"

"Yes, I'm fine. Just a bit shaken."

The cage was on its side but Tarragon stood up in it easily. Lily took the irin key and opened the small door, and the woodsprite ran out. Tarragon threw their arms around her, tears in their eyes.

"Thank you for freeing me."

"No thanks is necessary." Lily hugged him back, but only for a second before she got to her feet.

Lily stepped out of the cell and looked both ways down the hall. It looked exactly the same either way: long, narrow, and dimly lit with a few torches.

"Which way do we go?" Tarragon asked, standing beside her.

"I'm not sure," Lily admitted, and turned back to Aeterna. "Do you know?"

The irin shook his head sadly. "I was unconscious when they brought me down here."

"Well …" Lily bit her lip and nodded to her right. "This is the way the sonneillons came from."

Aeterna held onto Addonexus, leaning onto the unicorn for support. Tarragon hurried, moving their short legs quickly to match Lily's pace, and they walked right next to her.

"What was that?" Aeterna stopped short, so everyone followed suit. He tilted his head, listening, and Lily heard the footsteps behind them.

Tarragon reached up and wrapped their small hand around hers. "Someone's coming."

Without saying anything more, Lily began to run. She scooped up Tarragon to move faster, and Aeterna climbed up onto Addonexus. As they ran, the sound of footsteps behind them only grew louder.

CHAPTER THIRTY-THREE

LUX CLIMBED UP ONTO THE BRIDGE, smiling brightly at the two ogres guarding the door to Valefor's lair. They were monstrously large, even for ogres.

The taller of the two had only one eye, but they both had bulbous noses that seemed to take up most of their faces and gave the ogres their keen sense of smell. This was somewhat ironic since they reeked like dragon dung.

As a henchman for Valefor, Lux had dealt with the ogres before, but he'd never liked it. They spoke mostly in grunts and groans, and Lux had never quite gotten a grasp on it.

"Good afternoon," Lux said, doing his best to sound cheerful. The ogre with one eye scratched his head, looking as if he'd forgotten something, but the other one glared down at Lux. "I've come to ask for passage into the tower. I have business with Valefor."

Lux had been hoping that the ogres would be too ignorant to know that their Master wanted him dead now. Valefor had probably given them orders to kill Lux on sight, but that didn't mean that they would recognize him. They had a terrible time of distinguishing between humans, but they had guard duty because of their incomparable strengths, not their dim eyesight or low intelligence.

The ogres exchanged looks and made a few grunting sounds. Through their legs, he could see Wick sneaking up onto the bridge. She slid behind the

189

ogres, but if she tried to open the door, they would
hear and turn on her. Gula was on the opposite side of
the bridge, waiting until the ogres moved so he had
enough room to climb up.

The one-eyed ogre began to sniff and look around
as Wick rummaged in her satchel. The scent of
toadstool was strong on her, so Lux hurried to distract
him.

"Look, guys, I'm one of Valefor's servants," Lux
said, speaking loudly so both ogres would look at
him. "You've let me in here a thousand times, and if I
don't get in there now, the Master is going to be
furious."

"Master?" the one-eyed ogre grunted and
scratched his head again.

"Who you?" the other ogre asked and pointed at
Lux.

"Me?" Lux stalled since Wick still hadn't gotten
her potion out and Gula hadn't been able to climb
onto the bridge. "You know me! We're practically old
friends here! How can you not remember me?"

"Friend?" the one-eyed ogre asked, and his
comrade shook his head, clearly annoyed.

"Who you?" the ogre asked again, only angrier
this time, and he took a step forward, showing Lux
that he meant business. That gave Gula enough room
to climb onto the bridge.

"I'm, uh …" Lux fumbled, watching as Gula
nimbly pulled himself onto the bridge. "I'm… Ava.
Avaritia."

"Ava?" the one-eyed ogre questioned, then
frowned. "No, I know you. You Lux."

"Lux!" The other ogre made his massive hands
into fists, preparing to smash down upon Lux.

"*Statua magnus!*" Wick shouted and tossed a vial of pinkish liquid onto the ogre. It splashed all over his leg, and at first, it seemed to do nothing more than irritate him.

He bellowed in anger, then tried to lift his foot to step toward her, but his foot would not move. His mottled green skin began turning gray and hardening like stone. It spread out all over his body until finally, he was a giant ogre statue.

The one-eyed ogre growled in rage and turned to attack Wick, but Gula charged at him. He slammed into the ogre with all his might. The ogre waved his arms wildly before falling backward into the moat.

"Come on," Lux said, running past the statue ogre.

The one in the water was down for now, but it wouldn't be for long. And his splashing and yelling would attract attention, like sonneillons or worse.

The massive door was opened by a crank to the side. Lux began turning it, but Gula pushed him out of the way and took over. He was stronger than Lux, and within a few seconds, the door was open far enough for the three of them to sneak inside.

Valefor's lair was very dark, very dirty, and reeked of brimstone. They stepped inside a small entryway with two narrow hallways leading from it, along with one staircase winding down, and another winding up.

"Where would he keep Lily?" Wick asked.

"His chambers, I imagine," Lux said, then glanced to Gula for help. "He's trying to convince her to marry him, right? That's the best place to seduce her."

"You'd know better than I would," Gula said.

"This way then." Lux pointed to the hallway on the left and hurried down it.

The hallway curved several times and split off twice as they went, and Valefor's lair was somewhat of a labyrinth. As Lux led the way through, he noticed Wick, sprinkling fairy dust behind them.

"What are you doing?" he asked.

"Leaving a trail of breadcrumbs," she explained. "This is made from dried fairy wings, and it's nearly invisible to the naked eye. But if I shine my wand on it, it'll light up, and show me the way out."

They heard footsteps of someone approaching, and Lux motioned for them to duck back in a hall. They pressed themselves flat against the wall as they could. A torch burned near them, and Wick took out her wand and blew the fire out with it. They were hidden in the shadows, and that was the best they could hope for.

Lux held his breath as the footsteps got closer. He even tried to will his heart to stop beating.

A pair of sonneillons walked past, whispering to themselves. One of them paused at the end of the hallway, only a foot from where Lux was hiding. The sonneillon cocked his head, listening.

"Stop wasting time," the other sonneillon hissed. "The Master wants to see us right away."

The sonneillon nodded, and they both continued on their way.

Lux let out a deep breath once the sonneillons were gone. After waiting a minute to be sure they were safe, Lux turned back out into the hallway only to be confronted by a goblin.

It was slightly larger than a house cat, which was why they hadn't heard it approaching. Goblins had a scream like a siren that would alert everything in the tower to danger, and it had leather wings folded on its back so it could fly off.

"Listen, we don't mean any trouble," Lux said, trying to reason with the little monster before it started its warning cry. He stepped toward it, and the goblin hopped back. It opened its mouth, preparing to yell, and it unfolded its wings so it could take off. "Hey, no, there's no need to scream."

The goblin leapt into the air, its wings beating furiously. But before it could get anywhere, Gula reached up and caught it around its throat, so it couldn't scream. It fought hard against him, clawing at him and making small squeaking sounds. To quiet it, Gula snapped its neck.

"Thanks," Lux said.

Gula tossed the goblin aside and followed him. It wasn't long before they heard something else approaching and had to hide in a crevice in the wall.

It sounded like hooves coming toward them, but it was too loud and heavy to be sonneillons. He heard voices, too. They were whispering. But there was a familiar voice among them.

"Lily," Lux whispered, and without thinking, he bolted out from the crevice.

"Lux!" Wick hissed and tried to stop him, but he was already gone.

He saw them a few meters down the hall. He barely registered the irin with the broken wing, the black unicorn, or the little green sprite. All he saw was Lily.

"Lux!" Lily shouted.

They embraced, their lips pressing together fiercely. It was hungry, intense, and brief. He wanted to look at her, but he didn't release her fully. He kept an arm on her waist, afraid to let her go, and he cradled her face as tears spilled down her cheeks.

"You're alive," she whispered. "I was certain you had died."

"What have they done to you?" Lux asked, touching at the fresh cuts on her face. His anger surged anew as he saw how Lily had been battered and bruised in their time apart, and again he was vowing to destroy everyone who had hurt her.

"I'm fine. I'm only glad you are all right."

He shook his head. "You're not fine. This shouldn't have happened to you."

She stared up at him, her hand on his chest, but her eyes studied him with a new wariness. "I know what you are, Luxuria. And I know what I am."

CHAPTER THIRTY-FOUR

LILY COULD FEEL HIS HEART, pounding under her hand, and his eyes were wide. But he said nothing after her confession, though the way he looked – shocked and scared – made her think that she'd made more of an accusation.

His arm was still around her waist, and his hand on her face. But there was a tense distance between them, one that came from the realization that they were never meant to be together.

"*Lily*," he said finally, helplessly.

"We don't have time for this," Wick interjected, and she stood right at Lux's side, as if she wanted to wedge herself between the two of them.

"Wick," Lily said in surprise. "What are you doing with Lux?"

"Rescuing you, if you'll let me," the witch said, sounding annoyed.

"More sonneillons could be along at any moment," Aeterna added.

Lux glanced over at the irin and nodded grimly. He let go of her, and his attention was now set on Gula and Wick. The witch latched onto Lily the moment she could, wrapping a protective arm around her shoulders and pulling her away from Lux.

"I will work on distracting Valefor, but he's going to keep coming after Lily until she takes her vows," Lux said. "You'll have to go as far as you can, as fast as you can."

"If you stay behind, Valefor will kill you," Lily protested.

"He's my Master. I need to face him," he said without looking at her. "And it's my fault you're in this mess."

Lily wriggled away from Wick, and she walked right up to Lux, so he'd look at her again. "Why did you do it?" she asked him. "Why did you save me? Why didn't you tell me the truth?"

"I didn't know you were a virtu, not at first," he said thickly. "And I didn't tell you what I really am because I knew we didn't have much time together and…" He lowered his gaze. "I never wanted to see the disgust in your eyes."

"Lux…"

The unicorn stomped and chuffed, growing impatient, and Aeterna tried to soothe him.

"He's restless inside Valefor's walls," the irin explained.

"Gula can lead you out of here," Lux told Aeterna. Then he looked to Wick. "Go now, and I'll make my way to Valefor."

"I'm not leaving you, Lux," Lily insisted. "Not after I just found you again."

Somewhat uncertainly, Gula started leading Addonexus away, with Aeterna and Tarragon riding on the back of the unicorn. Wick stayed behind with Lux and Lily, probably to protect her, and the witch seemed ready to drag her away kicking and screaming if she had to.

"You're being ridiculous." Lux shook his head. "I'm a peccati. You shouldn't care what happens to me or risk anything for me. I've lied to you. I've put you in danger."

"No." She stepped closer to him, her eyes unwavering. "You've probably done horrible things, maybe even things that I could never forgive. But I know there is good in you, more good than you even know. You are worth saving and you are worth loving. I'm not leaving unless you leave with me."

"Isn't that sweet?" Ira said with a laugh. "It's too bad that I'm going to have to finish the job I started back in the Necrosilvam."

CHAPTER THIRTY-FIVE

FROM THE CORNER OF HIS EYE, Lux saw Wick pull
Lily away, and he stepped between them and Ira. Ira
had snuck up on them, coming from the opposite
direction that Gula, the irin, the sprite, and the unicorn
had gone.

"Ira, you don't want to hurt her," Lux reminded
him and moved closer to his brethren.

"No, I think I do." Ira smiled, which was a rather
unpleasant expression on his stony face. "Valefor
wants her to suffer, to show her what life will be like
without him. I can do whatever I want with her, as
long as I keep her alive.

"As for you," Ira continued, stepping closer to
Lux. "I have direct orders to kill you."

"*Lux!*" Lily yelled behind him, but Wick
mercifully held her back.

"Wick, get her out of here!" Lux shouted.

Lily broke free from Wick and ran to him,
begging him not to risk his life for her. She held onto
Lux's arm, but he didn't look back at her. He had to
stay focused on Ira.

Wick grabbed Lily, but before she dragged the
princess away, while she was right behind Lux, she
slid her wand into the waistband of his pants, all
without Ira seeing.

"Good luck," she whispered, then she forcibly led
Lily away.

Ira barely seemed to notice that Lily had gone, nor did he seem to care that she had. The lair was a maze, and Ira likely assumed that Lily and Wick would be unable to find their way out.

"I'm actually glad that I didn't kill you earlier," Ira said as he and Lux faced off, moving in a slow circle around each other. "I can really savor it this time, without that girl screaming in my ear. It was good of you to send her away."

Lux smirked. "You know me. I've always been a thoughtful guy."

Ira threw a punch at Lux, and he dove out of the way, narrowly missing one of Ira's rock-hard fists in his jaw. Ira laughed at that, a deep guffaw, and asked, "So we're going to dance, are we?"

Lux reached behind his back and pulled out the wand. The unicorn horn felt strangely heavy and electric in his hand. He pointed it right at Ira's chest.

"What is that you have there?" Ira squinted at it, as if he really didn't understand what he was seeing.

"A powerful wand." Lux had never used a wand before, but he kept his cool and his arm straight even though it wanted to shake. "Leave now, and I won't use it against you. But if you take another step, I'll be forced to destroy you."

"I'll believe that when I see it," Ira said.

Then Ira moved quickly at Lux and stopped short. It was a fake-out charge meant to startle Lux, and it worked. Lux flicked the wand, but nothing happened.

Ira stared at him, waiting for the magic, so Lux shook the wand again. Still nothing happened, and Ira threw back his head and laughed.

Of course the wand wouldn't work for him. It was a unicorn horn, and Lux was a peccati with no training in sorcery. He had absolutely no idea how to make the thing work, except what he'd seen witches do before. Wick just held it and magic spewed forth, but apparently, there was some trick to it that Lux couldn't fathom.

"Dammit," Lux muttered and shook the wand again.

"Oh, that's rich." Ira tried to quiet his laughter. "That is just pathetic, Lux! Is that even a real wand? Or is that a twig you picked up outside?"

Ira was too busy laughing to be on guard, so Lux charged at him. But as soon as Ira saw Lux moving at him, he stopped laughing and righted himself. He swung at Lux, who ducked, rolling past him on the floor, and then getting to his feet and running on.

There was nothing in this part of the hallway to fight Ira with, so he had to go somewhere else where he could find something useful. Ira called Lux a coward but chased after him. He heard Ira's feet behind him, sounding like a stampede of horses rather than one man.

Lux found the door he wanted by smell, and he threw it open. The skinning room had the distinct scent of hot oil and cooking flesh. Valefor liked collecting the hides of his victims, and the skin came off much easier when boiled in hot oil.

The skinning room had about ten feet of ledge right inside the door, and then it was open to a giant vat of boiling liquid. It was kept hot by lava that flowed up from the surface. The room was almost unbearably warm, and Lux could handle heat very well.

A sonneillon stood near one side of the room, stirring the oil with a large pitchfork. Apparently, there was something in the process of being skinned.

"Oh, good choice, Lux," Ira said, sounding genuinely impressed as he strode into the room. "I couldn't have picked a better place for your demise."

"I was just thinking the same thing, except about you." Lux faced Ira and flashed him a bold grin, even though he had no plan at all.

Ira charged at him, but when Lux tried to move out of the way, Ira's big arm pulled him into a bear hug. He lifted him up so Lux's back was to Ira, and Ira clamped one arm around his throat, so Lux could barely breathe.

"When you hit the oil, make sure you scream a lot," Ira said, growling right in his ear. "I want to hear you die."

Lux flailed, kicking at him with both legs, and futilely pulled at the arm crushing his neck. It would be easier if he weren't holding the wand.

Then Lux realized he had the unicorn horn still clamped in his fist. Just as Ira stepped to the ledge, preparing to drop Lux into the boiling liquid, Lux thrust the horn back and stabbed Ira right in the eye. Ira screamed and stumbled backward, then let go of Lux.

Lux hit the ground gasping for breath, landing just at the edge. He had jammed the horn right into his brain, and Ira's body flailed on the ground beside him. Lux got up, yanked the horn from Ira's head, and then kicked his heavy body into the boiling oil.

"The Luxuria has slain the Ira," the sonneillon hissed and stepped toward Lux, its long fingers reaching out for him. Ira might be out of the way, but the sonneillon would still get quite the reward if he killed Lux.

Lux rubbed his throat and stepped back from the sonneillon.

"Oy!" someone shouted, and Lux looked away from the sniveling minion to see Ava sauntering into the skinning room. "What's all this then?"

Lux grimaced, because Ava had come in to finish the job that Ira had failed to complete.

The sonneillon turned to look back at him. "The Luxuria has slain the Ira," it repeated.

Ava glanced between the two of them, but he didn't appear all that upset or surprised. "Well, the Luxuria is clearly having a very bad day, so perhaps we ought to give him a break?"

The sonneillon tilted his head in confusion as Ava walked over to him. "The Master must punish the Luxuria."

"I know you feel that way," Ava said with an apologetic smile. "But I think the peccati have already been punished enough."

While the sonneillon tried to discern what he meant – and honestly, Lux was just as confused himself – Ava had reached it, and without warning, he kicked the sonneillon as hard as he could in the chest. The creature went flying backward, growling as it fell into the oil. It began to scream, but only for a few seconds before it died.

Lux looked at Avaritia, shocked but grateful, and smiled weakly at him. "Thanks."

"I've never liked the sonneillon or Ira," Ava said, as if that was an explanation and smiled over at him. "But you know, Lux, I never work for free."

"Ava, I don't have – " Lux started to deny he had anything to pay, but then Ava's emerald eyes bounced down to the bloody unicorn horn in his hand. "You still want this?"

"Yes, I think I would." Ava held his hand out to him. "In my experience, unicorn horns always come in handy."

"I suppose you've earned it." Lux sighed and gave it to him.

Ava smiled brightly and wiped the blood off the horn on his clothes. "Now if I can offer you one more piece of advice – get the hell out of here before Valefor dismembers you."

"Thanks, but I've got other plans," Lux said.

With Ira taken care of, that left him with only one thing to do: Find Valefor and stop him from going after Lily. Because as long as Valefor was alive, Lily would never be safe.

CHAPTER THIRTY-SIX

SCELESTUS WRINKLED HER NOSE and glared at her little manservant sitting next to her in the coach. Jinn stared up at her, simpering and wide-eyed.

"You disgusting little goblin," Scelestus said as they bounced around in the back of the horse-drawn carriage. "How dare you pass gas in my coach!"

"It wasn't I, My Queen," Jinn said. "I would never do such a thing!"

"Then what is that wretched smell?" she demanded, and she still wasn't convinced that it wasn't Jinn.

He shook his head. "I'm not sure, My Queen. Perhaps we are getting close to Valefor's lair."

"It's about damn time," Scelestus muttered. "We've been traveling in this cursed carriage for ages."

She leaned over and pulled back the curtains so she could peer outside. Valefor's red tower jutted up on the horizon only a mile or two ahead. Scelestus smiled and settled back in the seat.

Since she'd gotten word from Valefor that Lily and Lux had gone missing, she'd been unable to speak to him. She'd tried sending messages or speaking to him through her cauldron, but he was either ignoring her or too busy. Either way, Scelestus needed to make things right with him.

After years of suffering as the Queen of the dull Insontia, she'd finally found her way out. In exchange for that useless stepdaughter of hers, she would be granted eternal youth when she took the role of the Invidia. But since she'd been unable to deliver Lily to Valefor, she would have to find something else that he wanted.

"How do I look?" Scelestus asked Jinn.

"Ravishing as always, My Queen." He smiled up at her, and she sneered at him.

They rode the rest of the way to Valefor's in silence. The crunch of the dirt road under the horses' hooves changed to the wooden of a bridge, and then the horses stopped sharply. An ogre grunted outside, and Scelestus motioned for Jinn to get out. He only spoke a little ogre, but it was better than her. He'd have to make do.

Scelestus waited in the carriage, smoothing out her hair. She pulled out her pocket mirror and checked her appearance. Everything had to be perfect for when she met with Valefor.

"What is taking so long?" Scelestus shouted out the window.

Jinn hobbled back to the carriage and opened the door.

"I'm not completely sure, My Queen," Jinn said. "There seems to have been some trouble here earlier today. The ogre at the door doesn't want to let anybody in."

"Oh, for heaven's sake." She rolled her eyes and pushed Jinn out of the way. "I'll do it myself."

Gathering her dress, she climbed out of the carriage and nearly knocked Jinn down. The sun was beginning to go down, but the light shined brightly past the tower, nearly blinding her. She squinted and walked around to the front of the carriage.

A one-eyed ogre stood guard in front of the door, looking irritable and confused. Next to him was a statue of another ogre, and Scelestus looked at it curiously. Perhaps it was meant to be some sort of gargoyle and scare people away when they approached the door, although she didn't find it all that intimidating.

"You there," Scelestus shouted up at the ogre. "Let me in. I need to see Valefor."

"No pass." The ogre shook his head and grunted.

"He wants to see me," she lied.

"No pass!" The ogre shouted this time and balled his fists up.

"It's about the girl," she said, trying a different tactic.

"Girl?"

"Yes, the girl," Scelestus smiled and did her best to sound charming. "The girl Valefor has been looking for. I have information on her that Valefor would be dying to hear."

The ogre furrowed his brow in deep concentration. She sighed and waited, afraid that if she pushed him he would attempt to squash her with his fists, and she didn't want to hurt one of Valefor's guards. What kind of guest would she be?

The decision was taken away from the ogre when the door behind him slowly opened. It didn't open all the way, but it was wide enough for a thin man to slip out. His skin had a faint greenish hue to it, and his eyes were too large for his face.

"What's going on?" the thin man asked.

"Girl," the ogre grunted and pointed to Scelestus.

"I'm here to see Valefor." Scelestus smiled at the thin man. "I know something about the girl he's looking for. I'm sure he'd really love to see me."

"Who are you?" the man asked, narrowing his eyes at her.

"Queen Scelestus." She curtsied a bit when she said it, even though the man looked like he was way beneath her station. His clothes were dirty, and his hair was a mess.

"Ah." The man smiled broadly at her. "Yes, I'm certain he'll want to see you."

"I knew it," Scelestus said, and she beamed at that.

"Come with me." He waved her on, and she started following him.

"My Queen?" Jinn asked. He'd been standing next to the horses, but he stepped forward to go after her. "Shall I come with you?"

"There's no need," she said dismissively. "Wait here with the animals."

Jinn bowed his head. "Yes, My Queen."

"It was very lucky that I caught you at the door," the thin man said as he led her inside the lair. He took the downward winding stairs to the left.

"Yes, it does seem quite serendipitous," Scelestus said. She lifted up her dress and stepped carefully down. It was dimly lit, and the stairs were steep. "I wasn't sure that the ogre would let me in."

"He's had a rough day," the man explained. "We all have. I'm normally not around here that often. There's not that much for me to do. But Valefor has called us all back to his lair to help with the girl."

"She's quite valuable to him, then?" she asked.

He nodded. "Extremely. That was a rather nice carriage you had out there."

"What?" Scelestus asked, confused by his change of topic. "Oh, yes. It's nice."

"I'd like to get myself a carriage like that," he went on. "I don't think I've had one that spacious before."

"It is roomy," Scelestus agreed.

They reached the landing, and the man directed her to go into the room at the bottom of the stairs. She smiled at him as she went inside, expecting to find Valefor. Instead, it was an empty room, with nothing but a table and a few pots and pans around.

"What is this?" Scelestus turned back to face the man, and he closed the door behind him when he came in. He leaned up against it, locking it behind his back. "Where is Valefor?"

"He's attending to some business," he explained. "So I thought we could use the time to get to know each other."

"I have no business with you." Scelestus straightened and pressed her lips into a thin line. She'd come here unprepared for a fight, and all her potions and her wand were with Jinn.

"I think you do." The man stepped away from the door, smiling wider at her. "I'm Invidia." He reached into his belt loop and pulled out a long, jagged knife. "I heard you wanted to take my life, so I thought I would repay the favor."

Scelestus opened her mouth and began to scream, but nobody could hear her inside Valefor's lair.

CHAPTER THIRTY-SEVEN

UNDER HER BREATH, WICK CURSED herself for leaving Lux the wand. She'd given it to him because he needed a fighting chance to survive. After everything he'd done for her and Lily, Wick felt like she owed him that much. But she'd done it in the heat of the moment and hadn't been thinking.

She had no idea how to get out. The trail of fairy dust she'd left would be of no use to her since it wouldn't show up without the magic of the wand. She and Lily were running blind through Valefor's lair. And Lily wasn't even running that fast.

"Lily, come on," Wick said. She still hung on tightly to Lily's hand, afraid if she let go that the Princess would stop completely.

"We shouldn't have left him behind like that," Lily argued.

"It's what he wanted."

"But it's not right." Lily stopped and refused to go any farther, no matter how hard Wick gripped her hand.

"Lily!" Wick stopped and faced her. "I left him with my wand. He'll be all right."

She shook her head. "I can't leave him to die for me."

"If he dies, it won't be just for you." Wick put her hand on Lily's cheek, her eyes grave. "It's for the whole world. If Valefor gets you, we all suffer. This is about more than just you or Lux."

211

"But why should my life matter more than anyone else's? Why should he suffer when this is all my fault?" Lily asked.

"It's not your fault." Wick shook her head. "It's *his*. He chose this life in service of a daemon. And this, what he's doing for you, is far more honorable than anything he's done before. In return, you need to get out of here alive. Otherwise his efforts will be for naught."

Lily looked up at her, her dark eyes swimming with tears and guilt. "And I'm sorry that you're here, getting dragged into this."

"No, Lily, I should've been involved with you much sooner," Wick said. "I love your mother, and she loved you more than anything in the world. When she was with your father, I had to care about you from afar, but after she died, I should've found a way to get close to you. To help you prepare for who you were meant to be, and to protect you from your vile stepmother.

"But I was sad, and I was scared, and I chose fear over love, and I stayed hidden alone in a dark forest," she went on. "I am here now, though, and I need you to be brave. You have to be braver than I was, and you need to do the right thing."

Lily bit her lip, and Wick took that as a sign of a reluctant agreement. She took Lily's hand again, and they began running.

They hadn't made it that far when the grunting garble of an ogre voice echoed off the walls. The oversized shadow stretched across the hall in front of them, and it was only a matter of moments before the ogre rounded the corner and spotted them.

With nowhere to hide, Wick opened the door closest to her. She ran inside, dragging Lily with her, and slammed the door shut behind them.

"Well, isn't this a pleasant surprise."

As soon as she heard the voice, Wick's heart stopped in her chest. She'd never heard him speak, but she knew who he was instantly. She turned around slowly to see Valefor sitting at the end of a long, black table. A large bronze goblet was in his hand, and when he took a drink of it, it stained his lips blood red before he licked them.

For a moment, she could only gaze at him. Throughout her life, she had felt little to no attraction for men, and it wasn't even attraction that she felt for him now. Nothing that truly resembled lust or desire, but the perfection of his appearance was overwhelming.

"Have you changed your mind about my offer already?" Valefor asked Lily.

"*Run*," Wick commanded.

She stood in front of Lily, but as soon as the princess moved for the handle, Valefor appeared next to her, slamming the door shut. Wick blinked, making sense of how he had disappeared in a split second, and whirled around to see him smiling down at Lily.

"What happened to your lovely face?" Valefor asked the Princess. He reached up and ran his fingers along the scratches on Lily's cheek.

"Don't you touch her!" Wick shrieked. She grabbed his arm to pull him back, and Valefor turned around. His eyes blazed with fury, and he smacked her hard enough to send her flying across the room.

"Wick!" Lily shouted and reached out for her, but Valefor stood between them.

Wick lay on the floor unmoving, with blood streaming down her face.

CHAPTER THIRTY-EIGHT

"NOW, WHERE WERE WE?" Valefor turned back to Lily, smiling widely. "Ah, yes, your face." When he reached for her again, she twisted away from his touch.

"I know you are frightened, but I don't want to hurt you." Valefor held up his hands, palms out, like he meant her no harm. He took a step toward her, but every time he did, she took a step back. "I can heal all your wounds. I can make all your pain go away."

"I do not want or need your help."

"I know that you believe that." His tone went patronizing, like he was talking to a small child rather than his intended bride. "You're a very brave girl. Defying me like this takes some gall, I understand that. I even admire your spark. But don't mistake my admiration for weakness. I will get what I want, Castimonia."

Lily shook her head. "I have to give you my allegiance. It's not something you can take from me, not by force or by trickery. And I will never, ever serve you."

Valefor sighed. "I'll admit, that does disappoint me. It's so much simpler when you don't fight. But it's not as much fun." He smiled, and it was a predatory, enchanting thing. "And everyone bows before me in the end."

He stepped toward her, and this time she didn't move. She held her ground and glared up at him.

"Remember what I said earlier?" he asked. "I can take your pain away, but I can give it just as easily."

He raised his hand, like he meant to strike her. Lily winced, steeling herself for a blow that never came. Instead, he ran the back of his hand down her face, caressing her. Hot tingles rippled through her flesh, like a pleasant flame, and she recoiled.

"What did you do?" Lily put her hand to her face, and instead of the painful cuts, she felt only smooth skin. "You healed my scratches?"

"I took your pain away," he said. "And that is the last time I will do that until you agree to be my wife, to love me, to obey me, and to bend to my will."

"You know my answer."

"That I do. And I also know your weakness." He stepped away from Lily, walking backward across the room. "And it's not pain. It's your heart."

"My heart?" Lily asked, and her eyes widened as she realized he was moving toward Wick, who was slowly waking up on the floor. "*No*! Leave her alone! She has nothing to do with this!"

"Of course she does." Valefor bent down and picked Wick up by her throat. She clawed at his hands and made guttural noises. "She's what's going to make you accept my offer."

Lily ran at him. Wick shook her head, and Lily halted. She stood in the middle of the room, watching as Valefor choked her friend.

"Please, Valefor, I beg of you." Her eyes scanned the room, looking for anything with which to attack him. But other than the chairs that were much too heavy for her to lift, there was nothing.

She had *nothing*.

"There is one way to stop this, my darling, and you know what it is," Valefor said. "If you accept now, I'll stop. I'll let her go free, and I'll even order my minions to leave her alone. She'll live a long, happy life. And all you have to do is say yes."

"I can't." With tears streaming down her cheeks, Lily shook her head and looked at Wick. She could see the pain and fear in the witch's eyes, and it broke her heart to be unable to stop him. But how could she, if that meant that the end of everything? "I'm so sorry, but I can't."

"You leave me no choice then." Valefor sighed. "I'm going to have to kill her."

CHAPTER THIRTY-NINE

LUX'S WORST FEARS WERE CONFIRMED when he heard Lily screaming. He raced down the hall and threw open the door to Valefor's chambers.

"*Stop!*" Lily wailed when Lux came into the room.

Valefor held Wick up by her throat, her feet churning the air below her. In an attempt to save her friend, Lily had grabbed onto Valefor's arm. She was pulling with all her might, and the daemon was unmoving.

"Leave her alone!" Lux shouted.

"Lux," Lily said desperately.

"You stupid boy," Valefor growled and tossed Wick aside. She collapsed on the floor, coughing, and gasping for breath.

"Lux, go!" Lily shouted. "He will torture you if you stay!"

"Actually, I am happy to see you." Valefor grinned at him, and the flames roared up for a moment, burning green and purple before dying down.

"I won't let you hurt them," Lux said, standing tall.

"That's fine." Valefor walked toward him, and Lily grabbed onto his arm again, trying to stop him. He knocked her back, so she fell to the floor. "I don't need to hurt the witch anymore." He smiled wider. "No. I'm going to hurt *you*."

"Lux! You need to run!" Lily got to her feet.

"I won't leave you again," Lux insisted and kept his eyes locked on Valefor.

"You picked the wrong time to become honorable," Valefor said, glaring down at his former minion. "If you'd only waited a day or two, until this was all over, you could've helped me rule the world. Your life would've been free of all pain and suffering. You'd never have to feel anything again. Isn't that what you always wanted?"

Lux shook his head. "Not anymore."

The daemon pulled his arm back and struck Lux so hard he went flying into the fire.

"No!" Lily yelled. She ran at Valefor, hitting him over and over again in the chest, but he only laughed at that.

"I bet you're going to be so much fun on our wedding night," he said, and he grabbed both her fists, nearly crushing them in his. "But right now, I need you to stop, because I have work to do."

He threw her aside, and she landed near Wick. Wick crawled over to her and wrapped her arms around her.

Lux walked out of the fire, his pants in tatters from the flames. His strides were long and purposeful, and his fists were clenched at his sides. He went right up to Valefor, and he hit him in the face with a burning hot coal, pressing it into Valefor's eye.

Valefor groaned and held his face, and Lux punched him again. But Lux didn't get in a third hit. Valefor recovered and knocked Lux down. While Lux lay on the ground, Valefor kicked him in the side over and over.

Lux didn't even try to fight back anymore. He couldn't. He lay on his side, doing his best to shield himself from the blows as Valefor pummeled him.

From the corner of his eye, Lux saw Wick and Lily making their way toward the door. To stop them, Valefor picked up Lux and threw him — his body slammed into the door and fell to the ground.

"Lux!" Lily broke away from Wick and ran to where Lux lay crumpled.

He didn't open his eyes when she reached him. He didn't even move.

"Lily, you should go," he whispered, his voice barely a sound.

She caressed his face, and he put his hand over hers and his eyes fluttered open. "If you die tonight, then I die tonight."

"No, you *must* live." He coughed, wincing with pain. "I'm sorry that I hurt you."

"None of that matters now," she assured him. "I love you, Luxuria."

Valefor laughed behind them, making promises that Lux's death would be slow and painful, but neither of them really heard him. They were focused solely on one another.

"I know." Lux squeezed her hand. "And I love you. No matter what happens here tonight, I want you to know that. My heart, my life, they belong to you."

Lily bent down, kissing him softly on the lips, and the whole room began to shake.

"You fool!" Valefor shouted, his voice becoming more of an animal roar than human. "What have you done? You've ruined everything!"

By then, the room was shaking too much for them to ignore. Lux craned his head to see Valefor standing and howling. The flames around the room nearly reached the ceiling, and the walls began to crumble. Large chunks of the tower were falling around them, as if it were raining boulders.

"We have to go!" Wick yelled and ran over to them.

She and Lily helped get Lux up. He leaned on both of them and moved as fast as his battered body would allow. Wick got the door open, and they hurried out just as the ceiling came down.

CHAPTER FORTY

"WHAT IS HAPPENING?" Lily asked.

"I don't know!" Wick shouted to be heard over the rumbling of the tower.

In the hallways, everything was chaos. All of the horrible creatures that worked for Valefor were trying to make their escape, but most of them ended up crushed under falling debris. Lux tried to give Wick and Lily directions on how to get out, but blood was streaming into his eyes and he couldn't see very well.

As they were running, the floor gave out in front of them. A sonneillon had been racing past them, and he barely grabbed onto the jagged edge of the floor. Lily peered over the edge, and a mile below them, hot lava bubbled up. The sonneillon's grip slipped, and he fell back, screaming as he tumbled to his death.

They turned around to go the other way, but the ceiling crashed down, blocking their path. Through the new hole overhead, they could see sky above them. It had turned a dark red, and it was filled with black smoke.

"What do we do?" Lily asked.

"We climb."

Wick started up the huge chunks of rock that blocked their way, but she slipped almost right away. The constant quaking made it impossible to get a grip. She tried again and slid back down to the ground.

With tears in her eyes, Wick shook her head. "There's no way out."

Lily sat down on the ground next to Lux. He sat up the best he could and wrapped both of his arms around her, so he could shield her from anything else that came.

"Take my hand!" a familiar voice said, and Lily looked up to see Aeterna floating above them.

His wings were completely healed, as was the rest of him. In fact, he didn't show any signs of his earlier wounds. He'd flown in through the hole in the tower, and he held out his hand for Lily to take.

Lily was too stunned to react, so Wick took his hand first. Then Lily got up and grabbed onto him, wrapping her arms around Aeterna's neck. With his other hand, he picked up Lux.

"Hang on tight," Aeterna said, and then he was flying out of the tower, his wings beating hard and fast.

Soon they were soaring high above the world, the crumbling tower below them. Lily clung onto him, afraid of falling, and she saw Lux doing the same.

"What's going on?" Lily asked, her face pressed into Aeterna's chest.

"There's someone you need to meet," Aeterna said, and then flew up higher, past the clouds into a blinding white light.

CHAPTER FORTY-ONE

LILY DIDN'T REMEMBER HOW SHE GOT THERE. One minute she was in Aeterna's arms in the clouds, the next her feet were touching the grass. A brilliant white palace sat before her in the center of a green island. Crystal- clear water sparkled around it, and the sun shone down warmly on her.

The grass felt amazing on her bare feet, much softer than grass usually did. In fact, she felt better than she had before. All the aches of her body were gone, and when she looked down, she saw no evidence of her wounds. Even her tattered dress had been replaced by a new, beautiful, white gown.

"*Lux.*" Lily remembered in a panic that she hadn't been alone and looked around frantically.

Both Lux and Wick were standing behind her, their confused, dazed expressions matching her own. Wick looked at her arms with amazement. Like Lily, they were free of any marks from her earlier fights. Wick's worn dress was replaced with a lovely new one, and her hair had been pulled back in beautiful curls.

"Lily," Lux said.

He had been fixed and cleaned up, and he looked so stunningly handsome, it was hard to believe he was real. His eyes were so brilliantly blue, and his smile radiated. Lily ran into his arms, and they felt strong around her.

"How is this possible?" Lily asked.

225

"I don't know." Lux looked on with the same awed expression as she had.

"Did we die? Is this the afterlife?"

He furrowed his brow. "I don't think I can get into the same place that you can."

"This isn't the afterlife," Aeterna said. He stood on the steps of the palace, and he waved them on. "Come on. She's waiting to see you."

"Who?" Lily asked.

"Luminelle."

Lily and Lux exchanged a look, neither of them really understanding what this meant or what had happened. He took her hand, and they started walking after Aeterna. Wick didn't follow, so Lily turned back to her.

"Wick, come on." Lily held out her hand, and Wick came over and took it. She squeezed it and smiled before they all walked to the palace.

There was no door to Luminelle's palace. The steps merely went up to a wide entrance between tall pillars. Beyond that, it opened into a white marble hall. Music played softly throughout, though Lily couldn't see the source of it.

"How did we get here?" Lily asked Aeterna as they followed him.

"I brought you here, of course," Aeterna smiled back at her over his shoulder. "People often don't remember the journey, at least not the first time. It's too much for senses to bear."

"What is?" Wick asked. "What have you done with us?"

Aeterna laughed. "Don't look so worried. You were simply healed along the way."

"Along the way to where, exactly?" Lux asked. "I know it's Luminelle's palace, but where is that?"

"It's not located on Cormundie, not in the sense you know it," Aeterna replied. "But don't worry about it. You're here now, and you're safe."

As they reached the end of the hall, they came to a rotunda. Lily could see the back of an irin, her golden wings spread out wide. Light streamed in from an open ceiling, letting the sun shine right down on her. Blue and white flowers filled the room, and the irin appeared to be attending to a plant.

Aeterna stopped and motioned for Lily, Lux, and Wick to continue on without him. Before she went in, Lily turned to face Aeterna. She reached out and touched his wing, the one that had been broken.

"How did you find us?" Lily asked, running her fingers over the silkiness of his feathers. "Last I saw you, you could barely even walk, let alone fly."

"Addonexus took me far enough from Valefor's that I could summon help," Aeterna explained. "Valefor's dark magic cloaked his tower in a haze, so I couldn't reach out to my fellow irins. Once I was out of range, Luminelle sent several irins to help me. They healed me, and I came back for you as soon as I was able."

"Did the irins do that to Valefor's tower?" Lily asked.

"No, that was you," Luminelle said from the rotunda, and Lily looked back at her.

She was more exquisite than any man or woman Lily had ever seen before, even Valefor. Her hair was the color of shimmering ebony, and her skin was tawny and smooth. She seemed to radiate light and love. Her beauty was almost too much to bear, and Wick actually bowed down before her, unable to stand it any longer.

"Me?" Lily asked in a voice that sounded too small to be her own.

"Well, no." She smiled and gestured to Lux. "It was your friend, Lux."

"What?" Lux asked. He tried to hide it, but Lily could hear the soft quake in his words that he was as intimidated and awed as Lily. "No, I ..." He lowered his eyes, shielding them from the irin's luminance. "I didn't do anything."

"Oh, but you did." Luminelle motioned for them to come forward. "Don't be afraid."

"How did I do anything?" Lux asked. He took Lily's hand again, and they approached Luminelle together. Wick waited near the outside, bowed down on the floor by Aeterna.

"You loved her," Luminelle said simply, as if that explained it all.

Lux shook his head. "I don't understand."

"She's not yet the Castimonia, but she is of irin blood," Luminelle said. "She is my great-great-great-great-great-granddaughter, and had she taken her vows, she would be the seventh Castimonia to walk the kingdoms of Cormundie."

"I would've been?" Lily asked. "I won't be the Castimonia now?"

"Things have changed," Luminelle said, then corrected herself. "*Things are changing.*

"Valefor wanted Lily to serve him, to give her allegiance to him," the irin explained. "If she had done that, he would've won, by turning a virtu to his side. Even if she wasn't yet fully realized as one, because of her irin blood and her pure heart, it would still be the same. He still would've corrupted one of our own, thus making him — and his side — more powerful.

"But instead of the virtu vowing to serve him, you — a peccati, the minion of evil — had vowed yourself to her." Luminelle motioned from Lux to Lily. "When you pledged your heart and life to her, you gave up Evil for the side of Good."

"When you told me you loved me," Lily's eyes widened when she looked at Lux, "you saved the world."

"I …" Lux shook his head, unbelieving. "But if you knew all this, if you knew that Valefor would go after her, why didn't you intervene? Why didn't you just stop him?"

"Because that's not how it works," Luminelle said. "We can't interact directly with each other. I cannot fight Valefor or set foot on his grounds, and the same holds true with him. You had to solve this on your own."

"But if Lily was so valuable, why didn't you have irins guarding her?" Lux asked. "She never should've been allowed to leave with me."

"We didn't know how important she would become in all of this," Luminelle said. "She's not the first virtu child born on Cormundie, but she was the first to lose her parent before she understood what she was. When the time was right, I planned to meet her to explain what she was, but I was too late."

"Why hadn't Valefor already won?" Lily asked. "When my mother died, wasn't there one fewer virtu on Cormundie than peccati? Hadn't Evil already outweighed Good?"

"No, because you were still there," Luminelle said. "You still had the irin blood and the Castimonia heart."

"What if I had died?" Lily asked. "When I was a baby? Or if my mother had died before she had me? What then?"

"Then the Luxuria would've lost all his powers." Luminelle gestured to Lux. "If a virtu dies, then the corresponding peccati loses his powers. Otherwise Valefor would've slaughtered all the virtus a millennia ago and declared himself winner. The Evil could only exist if its Good counterpart did as well.

"The same goes for the peccati," Luminelle went on. "When they died or gave up their powers, Valefor had until the sun set on the next day to find a replacement. If he didn't, then the virtu would lose her abilities. You've killed Ira, and now Pazentia is at risk of losing her abilities."

"So… is that it then?" Lily asked. "We've won? Valefor is slain?"

"Not exactly," Luminelle said carefully. "A battle has been won, but the war yet rages. Valefor isn't dead, but he has been banished from Cormundie and confined to his palace in the nether realm."

"How do we vanquish him?" Lily asked. "What can we do to win?"

"You needn't worry about that now," Luminelle said. "You have done well, and you have earned your time to recuperate."

"What does that mean?" Lux asked.

"Well, I suppose, you should work on being happily ever after," Luminelle said.

CHAPTER FORTY-TWO

AETERNA RETURNED THEM TO INSONTIA, and the kingdom seemed brighter than it had ever been before. In the pastures outside the palace, Lux saw his stallion Velox running alongside the royal horses, as if he'd somehow known that he'd be returning here.

Just outside the palace doors, Aeterna set down Lux, Lily, and Wick.

"Would you mind giving me a lift into the Necrosilvam?" the witch asked the irin once Lily had finished thanking him again.

"No, you can't go just yet!" Lily was appalled and grabbed Wick by the hand. "You have saved my life, and you were a dear friend to my mother. You are a part of my life now, and I want you to meet my father and my nursemaid Nancilla."

Wick smiled at her. "If that's as you wish."

"It is," Lily said enthusiastically. "Oh, and Polly and Poppy! They are the cutest mice you'll ever meet, and I'm certain that you'll love them." She turned back to Lux. "You both will."

Lux smiled, because she looked so happy and excited, and he couldn't stop himself. Her infectious joy was almost enough to overwhelm his trepidation at meeting her father. "Well, we'll see what the King thinks of me."

"He will love you because I do," she said with a conviction that made his heart flutter. "But he and Nancilla must be so worried since I've been gone.

They will be so happy to see me and to meet you both."

"If you don't need anything more from me, I should be on my way then," Aeterna said. "There is much work to be done right now. Cormundie is changing."

"When will I see you again?" Lily asked.

He gave her a solemn smile. "Soon. You'll have work to do, too." His dark eyes went to Lux. "As will you. But you've both earned a bit of respite for now."

"Thank you." Lux shook his hand, and some part of him still couldn't believe that this was all happening. He was shaking hands with an irin, and he'd fallen in love with a Princess and a virtu.

"Don't thank me quite yet," Aeterna said with a warm laugh, and then he took flight, his large wings carrying him high in the sky.

They watched him go for a moment, and then Lily and Wick started toward the palace.

"Lily." Lux took her hand, and she stopped and looked back at him.

"What?" she asked.

He pulled her into his arms and kissed her passionately. Her lips were cool and hungry, and she trembled against him. Her hand went to the back of his neck, and he felt her finger twirl around his hair, sending delighted shivers through him.

.

Maps

Tristitia

The Seven Fallen Hearts Saga

The fairy tale continues . . .

Coming Early 2022

www.HockingBooks.com

ABOUT THE AUTHOR

AMANDA HOCKING is the author of over twenty-five novels, including the *New York Times* bestselling Trylle Saga and the indie bestseller My Blood Approves. Her love of pop culture and all things paranormal influence her writing. She spends her time in Minnesota, taking care of her menagerie of pets and working on her next book.

To learn more, please visit www.HockingBooks.com

Made in United States
Troutdale, OR
01/21/2024

17054513R00152